I DON'T KNOW HALF OF WHAT I THOUGHT I KNEW!

?

Other books by Evelyn Taylor Stamps

Children's books

The Adventures of Herman Ant Private Detective
and His Trusty Sidekick Flysworth Jones

Mopit and the Utopia Forest

The Adventures of Herman Ant Private Detective
and the Blended Community

Roscoe and Friends:
Plight of the Homeless Dogs

Novels

When Love Was In Our Hearts

To Begin Again With Worn Out Tools

Darsula

The Price of Silence

Love Beyond Boundaries

Love Won't Let Me Wait

It's Not Too Late to Dance

*All books are available in Print and Digital formats
Purchase online or by contacting the author*

I Don't Know Half of What I Thought I Knew!

?

Evelyn Taylor Stamps

Edited by Shelia E. Bell
sheliawritesbooks@yahoo.com
www.sheliawritesbooks.com

Hello Readers,

I have finished another book! God has blessed me and allowed my mind to remember and to write. I thank you for being faithful readers. Of course, I am grateful to my spiritual leader, Reverend O.C. Collins Jr. and my Bethlehem Baptist Church family. They were there when my first book, "Herman Ant Private Detective and His Trusty Sidekick Flysworth Jones" was written.

I especially want to thank my children. Cynthia, Pamela, LaMar, Kenneth, Michael and my sweet Hattie, I want you to know that your love and support means everything to me. I love each of one of you and I thank God for you.

My brother asked me if I was overdoing it because this is my twelfth book. "No," was my reply. Each book has a message. This book explores the many things I thought I knew and discovered I didn't know. It is about change, everything changes but change itself. How do we face those changes? There is no manual that instructs us how to grow old, what rules exist, or what guidelines are necessary for that journey.

If God says the same, on June 10, 2020 I will be eighty-four. I am the mother of six children, sixteen grandchildren, almost forty great-grandchildren and a great-great-great grandson. I was not privileged with the knowledge that each of their issues, good fortunes, and mishaps could impact my life, my highs, my lows, and my peace of mind. Each is a ripple, like those caused by stones tossed in a stream or river. Countless ripples continue endlessly.

Evelyn

Who is That Person Staring Back at Me in the Mirror?

What do you do when you wake up one morning and realize you don't know what you thought you knew about so many things in life? Hannah Steele sat up in bed. There she was again, fighting with her overly active imagination. She had noticed for several years that certain things were out of sync. One thing she noticed was the old lady in her mirror. She couldn't believe she had gotten that old. Where did the years go?

What happened to the time in her life when she thought she had all the answers?

She thought for a while and realized the questions are the same, the answers are the same, the surprises that life throws in her path are the same. The thing that changed was her ability to handle those changes that were thrown in her pathway. When you think you finally have the answers no one is asking the questions.

She referred to herself as an *antique teenage*r. That reference reflects age. It's those moments when she realized that what seemed recent usually happened twenty or thirty years ago.

Age does not necessarily determine her value but it determines her ability to do certain things, many which declined as she aged.

What if there was a danger. How fast could she run from the situation? Could she run? When was the last time she ran?

That was an example of what she thought she knew. She didn't know if she could still run. There was a time she knew the answer to that simple question. As she aged, she realized so many of her skills changed.

Her hearing had diminished. Her eyesight was dimmer. Her steps slower and her memory comes and goes. Body parts hurt for no apparent reason and the stairs are longer. When did the vacuum cleaner become so heavy?

She had to step up her game. If she had questions, she asked them—if she remembered (smile).

When she asked questions, sometimes young people looked at her like she was speaking a different language. Was she?

It hit her like a ton of bricks one day. Those things she once thought were incased like cement in her brain were not! She thought she would always be in control. She had no idea that time often erases control. She came to the realization that she didn't know half of what she thought she knew!

No one said to her, "Listen, the time will come when your sharp memory may not recall your own name. You may start to notice a strange face in your mirror. That relationship you had with your children may change. You were aware of death, but now it's a constant visitor. One day you may even have to give up driving! Will you understand why?

So many things in life change as the clock of life continues ticking away. Hannah may not know half of what she thought she knew but she did know this—she is blessed. She was still living the life God blessed her to live. Growing old ain't for sissies, but it ain't too bad either.

1

Hannah Steele breathed in and out deeply. She sat at her kitchen table and waited for her coffee to finish brewing. Shaking her head, she willed herself back to the present moment but her mind drifted again. Who was she? She had undergone many changes as she continued the aging journey.

Hannah was in her early eighties, the mother of five children and one wonderful daughter by divine intervention. She had a plethora of grand and great-grandchildren and one great-great-great grandson. Married four times, Hannah was now a widow. Her first husband was the father of her five wonderful offspring. Husbands two, three, and four were loveable memories.

She looked around her bedroom. There were clothes everywhere. Clothes she had taken out of her closet when she dressed for church. One mind suggested she get up and place them back in the closet, but that was too much like work.

Hannah was not a spotless housekeeper. Her aged body had certain things it enjoyed doing. Housework was not one of them. When she was younger, she had been a collector of things. When she was raising her children she would often look for bargains because they were always outgrowing things. The habit had continued long after she was done raising them. Her excuse now for 'collecting' was she was always working on some project or other—true.

Hannah was a writer, a published author of a number of entertaining and fun books pertaining to living life as senior adults.

Hannah was pleased with her life. She was healthy, reasonably attractive, and financially *ok*. Yes, Hannah was perfectly content with her life. Self-contained, Hannah was focused on living life to the fullest, following her own agenda, and cultivating, not reinventing, herself. She was sure of who she was on the inside and was naturally sure of herself on the outside.

She had gotten up early, something Hannah did from time to time. It no

2

longer bothered her that the other side of her bed was empty. She called the shots in her life. If she found herself sleepy she went to bed or took a nap. If she wanted to get up at three o'clock in the morning and work on a project, she did just that.

Every choice she made was basic to her. By taking care of herself in ways both large and small, she was free to take care of others, if necessary. She was free to focus on real living rather than rushing through the essentials. She understood that the smallest gesture is a choice, a purposeful selection.

Life had taught her that the intimate details of her life were too valuable to toss carelessly aside. She was, by nature, non-confessional.

"Keep your business to yourself. If you don't spread your business *in* the wind, you won't meet it *on* the wind," her grandmother often warned Hannah when Hannah was growing up.

Following her grandmother's advice, Hannah was careful about gossip. Hearing about the misfortune of others was not her forte. No, Hannah was discreet, always making an effort to think before she spoke.

The doorbell rang, startling her out of her thoughts. "Who could be visiting so early? Has to be MaryLou," Hannah said aloud.

MaryLou was an early bird, usually rising well before the break of dawn. Hannah and MaryLou Strafford had been friends for almost forty years. They first met at juvenile court. MaryLou was a volunteer auxiliary probation officer at the time and Hannah was a juvenile probation officer for the Memphis and Shelby County Juvenile Court system.

Hannah pushed back from the kitchen table, stood up, and walked slowly to the door, remembering a time when she would sprint to answer that same door. As quickly as she opened the door, a gust of wind ruffled and scattered fallen leaves around. Fall was Hannah's favorite season. It was a lovely fall morning with a bit of chill lingering in the air.

Sure enough, just as she suspected, when she opened the door there stood MaryLou with a bright cheerful smile on her face, and holding what smelled like a basket of her freshly baked rolls. MaryLou loved to bake.

"Good morning, MaryLou." Hannah stepped aside so MaryLou could enter.

MaryLou came in unwrapping her brightly colored scarf from around her neck. Her cheeks were flushed from the bite of the northern wind. She removed her coordinated cardigan.

"How are you on this wonderful morning?"

"I'm blessed. Girl, what are you doing out this early?" Hannah smiled and reached for MaryLou's hand, thankful for their years of friendship.

Hannah closed the door and MaryLou followed Hannah to the kitchen.

"I was up before dawn and felt like baking. I baked a basket of rolls. Of course, I thought about my dearest friend," she said as she entered the kitchen and uncovered the rolls before placing them on the kitchen countertop. The aroma of freshly baked rolls filled the kitchen.

MaryLou's bone straight snow-white hair highlighted her sky-blue eyes that sat perfectly in her oval-shaped face. She was still very stylish, and a warm smile always seemed to radiate from her face.

"Thank you, MaryLou. I know they're delicious. They always are." Hannah smiled at the welcome sight. She loved MaryLou's homemade rolls.

MaryLou made herself right at home. She stood tip-toed and opened the cabinet above the sink, taking out two plates and two cups for coffee and rolls. Hannah always had a pot of fresh coffee brewing.

Hannah sat at the kitchen table while MaryLou busied herself with the baked goods and coffee. Hannah watched as she moved about before finally taking a seat at the table.

"MaryLou, do you ever wonder where the years went? I mean, we're old as dirt." Hannah laughed as she reached for a roll MaryLou had placed in front of her with a cup of coffee.

MaryLou sipped her coffee. "Girl, yes, I most certainly do. But what can we do about it? Nothing, Hannah."

"I know, but my problem is my mind doesn't register eighty-three, MaryLou. I don't *feel* like eighty-three. When I was a teenager, I used to think eighty was ancient. But now that I'm eighty, I don't think ancient, although I feel it a lot these days," Hannah quipped. "I have so many unanswered questions."

"I agree with you one hundred percent, but who's to answer our questions?" MaryLou asked. "Keep in mind, those with the resources and who would have the answers to these kinds of questions usually die before they share the information with us." MaryLou continued drinking her coffee and then took a bite out of her buttered roll.

Hannah continued talking. She was alert and excited about something. MaryLou could tell from the bounce in Hannah's voice. She knew this woman like the back of her hand.

"Statistics report seniors are living longer. There might be hope in the future for those who stand where we stand now."

MaryLou looked at Hannah, curiously. "So you've been reading and doing research again, huh? What are you working on now?" MaryLou grabbed another roll from the basket on the table and put it on Hannah's plate.

"These are so good," Hannah complimented. "Every time I think you can't out do yourself, you end up doing just that. Girl, you should open a bakery. You could be a millionaire."

MaryLou laughed. "Maybe when I was younger that would have been the perfect idea, but now all I want to do is bake when I want to bake, not because I have to bake. Anyway, I'm glad you're enjoying them. So, tell me, what are you researching now?"

"I'm looking for someone who can shed some light on aging. You know, like a sage," Hannah said.

"A sage? You mean sage like in the herb, sage?"

"No, not that kind of sage." Hannah chuckled.

"Then what's a sage?"

"A sage is a person who has attained great wisdom. The sage is old enough and wise enough to tell a person who is over eighty all of the delightful pitfalls to watch out for as we approach the one-hundred-year mark."

"Okay, I understand a person having wisdom. I have wisdom. You have wisdom. What's the difference with this sage person? And will they have knowledge about aging? Even if they possess the knowledge, will we remember what the sage tells us? You know what can happen to the senior memory; it can vanish like a puff of smoke," MaryLou said in between sips of coffee. "There one minute. Gone the next."

"You're right about that," Hannah agreed.

"I have a lot of questions," said MaryLou. "Like how do we grow old gracefully? I still can't figure that one out. Next, how do we handle the sudden death of a spouse or a child? I'm still not over John's death." MaryLou lowered her head as she remembered the death of her husband.

MaryLou bit into her roll and Hannah continued her mental investigation into aging. Aging was one of Hannah's favorite subjects.

Hannah got out of her chair, walked to MaryLou, and took MaryLou's hands in hers. "I'm happy you came by this morning. I always feel better after our visits."

"So do I." MaryLou noticed seriousness in her friend's mood and gave her a hug.

"MaryLou, do you ever talk to your children or grandchildren about aging and death?"

MaryLou closed her eyes for a moment before answering Hannah. "After the death of their father, my children evaded the issue like the plague," MaryLou said softly.

"My children change the subject and become evasive too," Hannah said.

"I think they find it depressing. If it depresses them, what do they think it does to us?" MaryLou thought of her beloved husband. "They're young with youthful encounters on their mind, like water skiing." MaryLou's mind briefly reflected on several family outings involving water sports.

"They can still do water sports," Hannah interjected. "Our aged bodies can no longer make all those technical moves."

"I know that's right," replied MaryLou. "Hannah, you seem a little on edge or distracted this morning. Is something particular on your mind?"

"I don't know. It's just that things are constantly changing. So many things are not what I thought they were."

Hannah had been in an emotional free fall since she received a letter from her son. She'd tried to push it from her mind but so far she hadn't succeeded. She continued her conversation with MaryLou.

"MaryLou, are you concerned about death?"

MaryLou was surprised at the question. Was Hannah a mind reader? That question bothered her a lot lately.

"When I was young, a little girl, I thought death only happened to old folks. Now I'm one of those *old folks*." MaryLou half smiled. "Do you wonder how it will happen? Will you simply keel over one morning while sitting on the john?"

"Yes, I think about it," Hannah replied. "One of my neighbors from way back, years ago, died in the bathroom. Her children heard a loud booming sound. They had to literally take the door off the hinges to get into the bathroom," Hannah voiced.

MaryLou frowned at that realization.

11

"After hearing that, I started leaving my bathroom door unlocked. That way, hopefully someone in my family could be by my side, assist me as I ebb my last breath or save my life," Hannah said.

"I rarely lock my bathroom door or any door in my house. I know this one friend whose brother had a stroke and fell out of his bed. His wife looked in his room and assumed he had left the house. An hour later he was discovered cold and stiff beside his bed. I said to my family when you look in my room, if I'm not in my bed check the floor," MaryLou explained.

"Well, I guess that's enough talk about morbid subjects."

"Yes, you're right. I want to think about living. Dying will come soon enough," stated MaryLou.

"You got that right." Hannah cautioned her mind to think on happier things. "These rolls are some of the best you've made." Hannah took a big bite out of the buttered roll and leaned back comfortably in the kitchen chair.

2

MaryLou understood Hannah was on a mission. It was as if she could read this woman's mind. Their relationship was that intertwined, much like a sisterhood. They knew each other's secrets. There had been so many changes in their lives over the years.

MaryLou's mind flashed to her husband who lost his battle with cancer a little over a year ago. She felt the wave of grief washing over her. Thank goodness Hannah's voice dragged her mind back to the present.

"What did you say?" MaryLou asked.

"I said, I don't go in the basement anymore to wash clothes. It's become too dangerous. The chance of falling down the stairs increases each year." A mental picture entered her mind. She saw herself crumpled on her basement floor. "My granddaughter does the laundry for me. She tells me to let her know if I need anything from the basement and she'll get it for me."

"Why don't you get one of those buttons you can push for help?"

MaryLou asked. "I've been thinking about getting one."

"I've thought about getting one, too. The commercials about them are on point. Have you seen the one with the woman at the bottom of the stairs curled over in pain?"

MaryLou chuckled. "Yes, I've seen it a thousand times. She's on the floor, but she has one of those buttons. She pushes it and someone comes on asking if she needs help. She tells the person she's fallen and can't get up. They tell her they're sending someone right away."

"But I was thinking about that too. What if the cord broke when she fell on it or what if it got buried under her crumpled body and she couldn't get to it? I guess I'm over thinking," Hannah surmised, shaking her head at her own thoughts. "In spite of that, I've still thought about getting one, but it's not free you know. There's a monthly fee."

"Yes, I know it's not free. I don't know if I want to get one. Paying for the button monthly would be just one more thing for me to keep track of," MaryLou said. "I already have enough on my plate. Hannah, why don't you put together a packet or booklet of some kind for senior citizens? You know one where we learn all about the do's and don'ts of aging safely."

Hannah giggled. "That's actually a good idea, MaryLou. It could be something like a to-do list for antique teenagers like us." She continued laughing and so did MaryLou. "Yep, a to-do list for the antique teenager."

"Hannah, you're kidding but I'm serious."

"I know you are, and like I said, it's a good idea. I could share a variety of tips and suggestions to benefit seniors like us. I can go into a number of subjects and explore various approaches to aging gracefully. We could even get together in a group. That way we could socialize while providing a means of contact with peers of the same age. There are frustrations and limits imposed on us seniors."

"Yes, a lot of senior groups are conducted by individuals who are the same age as our children. What do they know about those of us in our eighties?"

15

Hannah fussed. "Growing old ain't for sissies, you know."

"That's a true statement. It sure isn't for sissies. Then these younger people tell you stuff like *age ain't nothing but a number* or *you're only as young as you feel*. They can say things like that because they don't have our aching bones and joints. "MaryLou laughed. "At least not yet."

"I stand at the door of senility and it takes its toll," Hannah said. "My neighbor asked me one time why I was talking so loud. I told her it was because my hearing is not like it used to be and the hearing aids are amplified. And what about this one? This one is one of my favorites. It's when they ask what took you so long to open the door? I have to remind them of the stiffness and the fact I didn't hear the doorbell. I tell 'em it's called old age!" Hannah looked at her friend and both of them broke out in laughter.

MaryLou glanced at the clock on the oven. She had been at Hannah's house going on two hours. "My how quickly the time has passed." MaryLou stood up, walked over to the kitchen sink, and placed her plate and utensils in the sink.

"Don't forget about the medical field. There's plastic surgery for just about anything. Almost every body part can be replaced."

"But we are as old as the years have racked up," MaryLou countered. "Eighty-three comes with its share of stiff aching joints and a memory that's unbelievable."

"I know, right. Guess what? I found my cell phone in the refrigerator the other morning. I don't remember when I placed it there." Hannah smirked.

"What about friendship with the opposite sex? Many men develop shyness as they age," said MaryLou. MaryLou waited for Hannah's advice.

"I've developed a routine that works for me when it comes to approaching a man."

"What is it?" asked MaryLou.

"Okay, well, first I ask him how old he is. I want to know if they're at least seventy. I'm not talking to anyone younger than that. If they're at least seventy, I move on to the next question."

"What's the next question?" asked MaryLou.

"The next question I ask him is are you married?"

"What if they say yes, they're married? What do you do then?"

"I say, your wife is a lucky woman." Hannah laughed.

MaryLou broke out in laughter too, while setting the basket back down on Hannah's table. "What if they say they aren't married?" She continued a chuckle.

"If they say they're not married, I whip out my pad and ink pen and say, may I have your phone number?"

"Girl, aren't you concerned you might be considered a *cougar*, or being too forward?"

"No, not at all. When you're in your eighties like me and you, it doesn't stand on protocol. I do things decently and in order by first asking if they were married. Anyway, I would consider it a compliment if they thought me a cougar." Hannah laughed. "But so far, not one has hesitated giving me their phone number. I say I'm a lucky girl."

18

"And I say, I wish I had your nerve." MaryLou replied.

"It's not about having the nerve; it's about common sense. This life is not a dress rehearsal, MaryLou. We don't get a repeat performance or a do over. Nope, this day will not repeat itself. I don't know about you, but I'm not wasting a minute of my life."

"Hannah, if you can add happiness to your aged existence, I suggest you take advantage of it."

MaryLou walked toward the door. "I'm going to the nursing home to visit one of my friends. You know how much I enjoy listening to you, but I need to go. I don't want to be gone too long."

MaryLou picked up her roll basket with Hannah following.

Hannah removed MaryLou's scarf and sweater from the coat rack and gave it to her.

MaryLou put on her sweater, wrapped her scarf around her neck, and stood at the door.

Hannah opened the door and walked MaryLou to her car. The friends chatted a few more minutes before they embraced.

19

"Stop by anytime with another plate of fresh baked rolls, "Hannah said, stepping back as MaryLou opened her car door and got inside.

"I will. Have a good day, Hannah."

Hannah watched MaryLou until she was out of her driveway and into flowing traffic. She walked back into the house. Suddenly, she felt empty and lonely.

3

The phone rang while Hannah was tidying up the kitchen. She looked at the caller ID screen. It was Raymond Moss.

Raymond was one of the gentlemen Hannah befriended when she presented him with the series of three questions she told MaryLou about. Those questions sparked a friendship between Hannah and Raymond. He called Hannah every day.

Raymond was a distinguished eighty-six-year-old gentleman. He had been divorced for many years and lived alone in a *seniors only* apartment complex. He was a little shy of six feet tall, slender, with deep dark melanin complexion, cocoa brown eyes were set off by bushy salt and pepper gray eyebrows. His white hair was neatly trimmed and his face was clean shaven. He was definitely aging well.

Raymond and Hannah talked for several minutes while Raymond prepared breakfast for himself. "Listen,

Hannah, let me finish making breakfast and I'll call you back."

"Okay, sounds good. I remember what happened the last time we talked while you were trying to cook. You burned your food."

"Yep, I did. That's because I got distracted," Raymond explained. "I'll call you back as soon as I'm done."

♦

The kitchen chair scraped against the floor as Hannah pulled it out to sit down. She called Raymond after some time passed and he hadn't called her back.

Raymond picked up the phone on the first ring. "I knew it was you," he said. "You thought I had forgotten to call you back, didn't you?" He laughed in the phone.

Hannah laughed too, knowing he had forgotten whether he cared to admit it or not.

"Hannah," Raymond said as they talked, "I had thirteen sisters and brothers. I'm the only one left. The only one still living."

Hannah could hear the overwhelming sadness in his voice. It sounded like he was trying his best to maintain a tight control over his emotions.

"Were you close to your siblings?"

"Yes, very close," Raymond replied. "I grew up in a two-bedroom house. I remember having to sleep in a crowded bed with someone's foot near my head or waking up wet because someone urinated in the bed. Guess that's why I decided early on that I was not going to father a gang of children."

Hannah leaned back in her chair and listened. She enjoyed hearing Raymond talk. His voice was so magnetic, so hypnotic.

"A few weeks ago, I attended the funeral of my last sibling. I'm now officially alone," he whispered.

"But you have your kids," Hannah reminded him, wanting to ease his pain.

"I know, but I seldom hear from them. They're busy living their own lives. I can't say I blame them. They're both teachers. I'm grateful I was able to provide them with a quality education. It called for a lot of sacrifices on my part and on the part of their late mother too," he whispered. "Sometimes I think maybe I was a bad parent. But I did the best I knew how. I worked hard, made sacrifices for my kids so they could have the better things in life. Times were hard. Sometimes it was difficult providing for my family. I know I made mistakes," he murmured. "Plenty of them. My daddy never sat down and talked to us when I was growing up. I promised I would never be like him. I was always there for my kids. I never thought a time would come when I would feel so alone." Sadness rang in his voice.

His children's actions or lack thereof devastated him. He wanted to confront them, force them to own up to their betrayal. That's what it felt like—the ultimate betrayal. Yet, he loved them.

Hannah reminisced about the day when she and Raymond first met. She was with a group of seniors on their way to one of the local casinos for a day of fun gambling and eating at the casino buffet.

Hannah climbed on the crowded bus. She noticed a vacant seat, middle ways the bus. An aged gentleman occupied the other seat. Was he waiting for his companion? Hannah thought.

"Excuse me. Do you mind if I sit here?"

The man looked at Hannah and smiled. "Of course I don't mind, but consider yourself warned, I'm a naughty man," came a reply.

Hannah stared at him. "I beg your pardon?"

"Consider yourself warned. I'm a bad man," he repeated.

She stared before asking, "How old are you?"

"Eighty-four," he quickly answered.

She sat in the empty seat, leaned close to him, and whispered, "I think I'll take my chances."

Hannah and Raymond laughed and talked every mile of the trip. He told her he was a barber by profession. He was well known because of a unique method he developed for treating hair. He told her he had been interviewed a number of times by the local newspaper and television stations.

At the casino, they continued to enjoy each other's company. They ate and gambled together. That was the

25

beginning of their friendship. Today they were closer than ever.

The lull of his voice over the phone snapped Hannah back to the present. "Raymond, as much as we wish we could, we cannot change the past." She stared at the phone for a moment.

"What are you doing today?" She knew the answer to her question before she asked it. He was at the barbershop. He opened the doors every morning at seven sharp.

"I'm at the shop," he said.

When Raymond first told Hannah he still cut hair she was shocked. She thought a man of his age would have retired. He'd certainly paid his dues.

Raymond had taken Hannah to his barbershop one evening after hours. She was impressed when she walked into the quaint space. There were rows and rows of accolades hanging on the walls throughout the barbershop. Newspaper clippings, photos with celebrities, magazine articles, all lined the walls.

Raymond remarked, "Everything in here speaks of my life." He grew quiet for a moment. "I'm a master barber. I have customers who trust only me to cut their hair. I have a few guys whose houses I go to because they're homebound and unable to get out of the house."

"Do you realize how much that type of service means to those customers?" Hannah remarked. "I mean, you collaborate with others, you communicate effectively with different personalities. You know how to push back diplomatically when necessary." She hesitated for a moment, giving her words time to take root.

"I was so busy worrying about what I didn't have that I forgot what I had. I neglected to spend the time I should have with my kids." Raymond cleared his throat.

"Don't beat up on yourself, Raymond. Your life is meaningful. And you give so much to others. You are an excellent example for the younger generation. They may not show their appreciation now, but someday they will. You see, Raymond, there is a constant in the universe. That constant is change. Everything changes. People change, our children change. Everything but change itself. So clinging to thoughts you had

27

felt terrible because she was unable to put the things Alvin said behind her. The lack of communication with her child bothered her. When she thought she understood life and was at a happy place, this happened. Should she blame herself? Things changed but God does not change. Thank heavens for that.

She walked back to the kitchen and picked up a jar of pickles and attempted to open it and couldn't. That's another thing she did not know. How could she have known the time would come when she would be unable to open a jar! She had opened it without any effort. What would be next? She reached and got a jar opener from the cabinet, a special invention for seniors. She had seen the device in a catalog and she ordered one. It had teeth like things that you place over jars. It added traction and helped her turn the jar top to open it. When she first got the device, it took a while for her to see and understand the directions. She wondered if the manufacturer knew this invention was for the senior population. Why were the directions in such small print, and in such an unfriendly senior color? Red writing on a red background was almost impossible for most nearsighted seniors to read.

She put the jar of pickles in the refrigerator, turned off the light, and went to her bedroom. She stood outside her closet, deciding what to wear for her adventures for the rest of the day.

Hannah dressed in something casual and put on her favorite tennis shoes. She used to think that type shoe unfashionable, but safety and comfort before fashion these days. She applied insect spray to keep mosquitoes from biting.

They bit and she did not hear them buzz. She knew to swat the little pests because she heard them. Now she heard nothing but she itched for days. She was ready for her excursion in the park.

The phone rang. It was Raymond. "Hey, I just finished with my customer. I don't have another one until later this afternoon. Would you like to enjoy a light lunch and a visit with a favorite friend?"

"Sure, Raymond. That sounds like a good idea."

"Do you want to meet me at the park?" he asked.

She could kill two birds with one stone, do her walk, and have lunch. "Yes, I'll meet you at the park."

"Okay, I'll stop at Wendy's and get sandwiches and a frosty," he said. "I should be there in about thirty minutes."

♦

Hannah watched the pigeons scurrying around and the birds flying through the mass of trees while she sat on the park bench and waited for Raymond. Times like these, she enjoyed.

The park they met up at was located right up the street from where Hannah lived. It had a walking trail and a dog park for seniors who loved their four-legged companions.

Sitting on the park bench, Hannah observed young people throwing Frisbees for their dogs to catch. Both young and old made use of the newly paved walking trails.

Hannah, for no particular reason, looked to her left. As soon as she did, she observed Raymond strolling slowly toward her. She could tell from his gait, he was more than likely dragging or shuffling his feet. When she was a young girl she used to wonder why some people, mainly older people, shuffled their feet when they walked and always looked down. She learned later, through life, age and experience of her own, the reason they shuffled was because the tendons, ligaments and sinews in the ankle and foot had grown stiff and tight from age. As far as the reason for looking down, it was to prevent themselves from tripping over some object and falling flat on their face.

"Hello, there. And how are you doing?" Raymond had a Wendy's bag in one hand and a cup holder with two cups in the other.

"Hi, Raymond." Hannah blushed.

He sat beside her and kissed her lightly on the forehead. "Here you go." He passed the bag to her and removed a cup from the cup holder, passing that to her as well. "I hope you like tomatoes and lettuce on your sandwich. Oh, and I also told them to hold the onions."

"That's fine. Thank you," Hannah said, accepting the sandwich he pulled from the bag. "I hope you have your mosquito spray. You know they bite without buzzing these days," Hannah said as she took a bite of her sandwich, and placed a straw in her Frosty.

"Mosquitoes still buzz. You just can't hear them unless you have your hearing aids on," he said.

"That's possibly true," Hannah mumbled. One more thing she did not know. She didn't know her hearing could be enhanced by a pair of very expensive hearing aids. She enjoyed Raymond; they spent a lot of time together.

He gave her a loving nudge. "I'm grateful for your friendship. When I hear your voice on the phone my spirits lift," he said.

They sat reminiscing for an hour or so before parting ways. After Raymond left, she remained in the park for a while. Trees shed their leaves. The winter landscape was near. It was almost September. The words of a song came to mind, *"It's a long, long while from May to December. But the days grow short when you reach September.*

And the autumn weather turns the leaves to flame." She hummed the lyrics.

Hannah had brought nuts for the squirrels. She pulled the plastic bag from her jacket pocket, opened it, and began throwing some in the grass. Feeding the birds and squirrels further relaxed her, and gave her a sense of tranquility.

5

Spending the afternoon in the park enjoying the fresh air was refreshing. While sitting there on the park bench, Hannah thought of a lot of things that had transpired over her life. Her mind soon fell on her oldest daughter, Ruth. Ruth was a widow inundated with grandchildren. She worked with her grandchildren in church and brought them to visit Hannah faithfully.

Ruth did just about everything for Hannah including taking care of Hannah's car by checking the fluid levels and battery.

Hannah didn't know that life would someday reverse positions. It was as if Ruth was the mother, not the other way around.

Hannah drove herself wherever she wanted to go during the day . Ruth, however, drove Hannah around at night.

Hannah was thankful for her children, however she knew how that could change in a moment. She remembered when another friend of hers named Sharon Black lost her fifty-two year old daughter suddenly. Then there was MaryLou's husband who had died recently. Death, although a part of life, is usually always a shock.

Three years had passed since Sharon Black's daughter, Carol, died. Hannah could recall that grief-stricken visit as if it was yesterday.

Hannah parked her car and walked slowly up to Sharon's front door. A brisk fall wind was blowing and leaves danced on the ground. There was a winter chill in the air that day. In her mind, Hannah could see Sharon standing at the door as Hannah entered.

"Carol loved this time of year. She would decorate the porch with spider webs and all types of ghoulish things for Halloween. "Sharon remembered, tears forming in her eyes. " Hannah, I know we shouldn't question God, but I do. I ask him why he took Carol. She was special. There was never a day that she didn't call or come by. The last time she came she said she wasn't feeling well. She was having chest pains so I told her to go to the emergency room. I wanted to go with her but she told me she would be fine. She said it was probably trapped

37

gas or something. Two hours later I received a call from the hospital. Carol had fallen unconscious, went into cardiac arrest, and never regained consciousness. I never got the chance to say good-bye."

Remembering that day still hurt Hannah's heart. What would she do if something happened to her dear daughter, Ruth? What would she do if something happened to any of her children? She loved them all and would be devastated.

A gust of wind stirring leaves hit her ankles, danced around her feet, bringing her mind back to the present. Hannah's mind returned to her situation with Alvin, her son.

Hannah's mind cleared. When she looked up, she noticed a young woman walking in her direction and pushing someone in a wheelchair. The young woman stopped in front of a bench near where Hannah was seated.

A ray of sunlight projected the scene. Hannah was quite observant. Friends accused her of noticing everything.

The lady Hannah assumed was the person's caregiver sat on the bench after positioning the woman in the wheelchair next to her. Removing a book from her bag, the woman opened it and began reading. The light from the sun settled on her face.

Hannah saw a sad, forlorn expression on the face of the slumped woman in the wheelchair. Her body language spoke volumes. She wore her sadness like an outer garment. The briskly blowing wind didn't seem to faze her. Hannah wondered how that much sadness could exist in a human being. Did it creep like air seeping from a tire or was it like a slow leak you didn't notice because it was so gradual?

The lady didn't seem to notice Hannah. She simply stared into space. Her emerald green eyes had such a lost look. Her smooth complexion was that of a white person who aged well. Her beautiful gray hair had the appearance of a recent visit to a hair salon. Hannah imagined the lady was afforded all that money could buy. Yet, she seemed so alone, just sitting in that very expensive chair. It broke Hannah's heart. She felt compelled to say something. That was Hannah!

Hannah placed the peanuts back in her pocket, got up from the bench, and approached the lady.

"Hello, how are you? Would you like company?"

The lady's eyes met Hannah's eyes.

"My name is Hannah Steele. I come to the park often just to get out of the house and think."

There was no reply. The woman seemed on another planet.

"Are you alright?" Hannah continued speaking.

The lady sat up in her wheelchair. Her eyes blinked.

The caregiver never took her eyes away from the book she was reading.

"Are you alright?" Hannah asked again. Hannah glanced over her shoulder at the caregiver.

The woman in the wheelchair gazed at Hannah as if she was finally seeing her. Tears fell from her eyes.

Overwhelmed with compassion, Hannah sat on the bench next to the stranger. For a third time, Hannah asked, "Are you alright?"

The lady responded by reaching into her dress pocket, pulling out a piece of tissue, and wiping her eyes. "It has been such a long time since anyone actually talked to me. I mean other than my nurse or caregiver." Her ashened complexion showed some color. Her body adjusted itself. She sat taller in her wheelchair. Soon the woman was engaged in conversation with Hannah.

"Coming to the park is something different for me," the woman explained. She said her name was Rachel. Her son felt some fresh air would be good for her. He had asked Kathy, Rachel's caregiver, to bring Rachel to the park.

"I don't mean to pry but you look so sad," Hannah whispered.

Rachel looked at Hannah, surprised at the stranger's observation. Words tumbled from Rachel's mouth like a floodgate had been opened. "My husband died a year ago. It's been really hard for me to accept his death." Tears started flowing. The caregiver remained quiet, still reading her book.

"What was your husband's name?" Hannah asked.

"Harold. We were married forty–two years. He was my rock. He was such a gentle, kind, understanding man."

Hannah studied this woman. As she talked about her late husband, Hannah noticed Rachel's posture straightened and, her facial features softened a little.

"He had been ill for several years; congenital heart failure. The doctor's prognosis was grim, but I still prayed for a miracle. God took him home though. After Harold died, Luke, our youngest son, moved me into a home for seniors. He hired Kathy to take care of me. We come to the park so I can get some fresh air."

Hannah looked briefly at Kathy the caregiver. Kathy kept her eyes focused on the book she was reading.

"Kathy is nice. While she reads I sit in this chair and think about the blessful years I spent with my Harold," Rachel said sadly.

Hannah listened attentively as Rachel shared precious memories about her and Harold.

"I wish I could join him. It's so lonely without him. I wish I could fall asleep and not wake up," Rachel sighed. " I wish my heart would simply stop beating." Rachel sobbed.

Hannah moved closer, tenderly taking Rachel's hands in hers.

Rachel didn't resist the stranger's touch.

Hannah said as cheerful as possible, "Things will get better for you." Those empty words escaped her lips before she had time to think about what she said.

"How can you say that? What do you know what's better for me?"

"You're right, I don't know. But I wish I could help you. I wish I could say something to make you feel like living." Hannah stared into Rachel's eyes meaning every word .

"You say you were happy with your husband." Hannah searched for an approach, some point of contact. "Would he want you to give up and die?"

Rachel paused for several seconds, gazed into space, and replied, "No. He...he made me promise. Rachel heard his words as if he was sitting right next to her. *"You have your life ahead of you. Don't become bogged down in grief when I die."*

"Rachel," the caregiver's voiced interrupted the flow of conversation. The

43

young woman finally acknowledged Hannah sitting near Rachel. " I see you made a friend."

The attractive young woman closed her book and extended her hand to Hannah. "Hello, my name is Kathy."

"Hannah, "Hannah replied.

"Nice to meet you, Hannah," Kathy said and then focused her attention on Rachel. "Rachel, it's time to go. Maybe we'll see you again," Kathy said as she released the brakes that held the chair safely in place.

"It was nice talking to you," Rachel said.

"You as well," said Hannah.

Kathy waved at Hannah as she wheeled Rachel away.

Off in the distance Hannah saw the outline of Senior Villas where Rachel lived.

6

Hannah remained on the bench after Rachel left the park. She suddenly felt melancholy.

She stood up and stretched as she felt the effect of sitting on a hard bench for an extended period. The afternoon sun was now hidden behind clouds. It had been a long day.

Hannah's mind reflected to the letter she had gotten from her son. *"Mother, please know I am not angry with you. I have decided to be more concerned for my future. We will talk less on the phone."*

Just like the brisk wind tossed paper and small leaves from one place to another, Hannah's life was being tossed. Suddenly, she felt exhausted, drained of joy. Slowly, Hannah got up from the bench and reached into her pocket for any peanuts she had left.

She threw the rest of the peanuts to the birds and squirrels, grabbed her walking stick, and stood in place for several minutes. A slow take-off was necessary for her aged body. The walking stick was more for protection against some overzealous dog rather than for walking support.

She smiled when the sight of her house came into view. She had lived in this house for more than forty years. Her children, grandchildren, and several great-grandchildren had grown up in this house. Hannah walked up her back steps , unlocked the door, and entered the kitchen. The house was quiet. She hung her keys on the key rack, the first thing she always did when she walked into the house. No stopping. No distractions! Her mind recalled sheer panic the time when she misplaced her keys for weeks.

Hannah walked to the kitchen, got a glass of milk from the container in the refrigerator, and sat at the kitchen table. Her son's letter was still on the table. Staring at the envelope, she finally reached for it as if she had to build up courage first, opened it, and began reading.

The meaning was difficult to understand. She fought back tears, trying to delay depression. She recalled articles she had read in several magazines.

"Some change may look negative on the surface but one will come to realize that space is being created in their life for something new to emerge."

She recalled what she read about the shark. Sharks never stop moving. Change is like a shark in the ocean. Change never stops. Never sleeps. It's always moving.

The article she read also mentioned a river. The same river, although its waters are constantly changing, is still that river. Like that river, so is life. Life is the same although it is constantly changing. Family is the same family although it is constantly changing. Children are the same children although they are constantly changing.

Hannah kept that article to refer to again. MaryLou was right, she was always reading something.

Hannah had changed in many ways herself. Should she embrace a certain amount of detachment from her children as change and not take it personally? Was that a part of healthy growth? She held the letter in her hand.

She knew better. They had a special bond. She had done something to hurt him. Not intentionally. Never intentional, but something had occurred. What though?" she asked herself.

Alvin was the kind of individual who remembered everything in defined details. Her memory was no match for his. Talking to him on the phone or writing him letters only bogged her deeper in conflict with him. Lately, when she called him, her calls started going to his voicemail. Was he intentionally refusing her calls?

Hannah thought about her grandmother whom she often emulated when she was younger. Did her grandmother experience a troubled relationship with any of her children? She never heard her grandmother complain about anything. Her grandmother never said an unkind word about her mother or father. Her grandmother's motto was "If you can't say something good, then don't say nothing."

Hannah's mind replayed a recent conversation she had with her son. *"It was never my intention to hurt you," she had told him. He remained silent on the phone for several seconds. When he spoke, he said three words," Well you did."*

The kitchen clock chimed, dragging her back to the present. Hannah glanced around making sure everything was in order. After placing the dishes in the cabinet, Hannah took a stack of mail from the counter, and walked into the den to sort through it.

The phone rang. It was Ruth. "Hello, Mama. I'm just calling to tell you good night and that I love you. Have a good night's sleep."

"Thank you, Ruth. And I love you too."

After she hung up the phone, Hannah must have dozed off because the next thing she remembered was bending over and picking up the stack of mail from off the floor. It must have fallen off her lap when she fell asleep.

Hannah got up and walked to her front window. Darkness had settled in. She closed the blinds and returned to the couch and started sorting through the mail. When she was finished, she reached for the blanket on the couch and covered herself. She did that on many occasions. Sometimes she didn't feel like getting up and going to the bedroom so she would sleep on the couch. One of the pleasures of living alone and in peace.

7

Daylight streamed through the closed blinds. Hannah got up from the couch, stretched, and bent down touching her toes. She laughed to herself over the fact she could still touch them.

She fixed and ate breakfast, and then did a few things around the house. It had been several months since she'd heard Alvin's voice. Aside from the letter, no other communication had been made. She stopped calling him after her calls continued going to voicemail. Trying to talk to him right now was pointless.

Determined to keep her mind clear of depressing thoughts, she decided to finish some of her craft projects.

Hannah worked on and finished several things she had started. When she was done, she felt better. Staying busy always seemed to clear her mind.

Margo Smith, a member of her creative writing class, called Hannah. Margo and Hannah shared a friendship although Hannah was almost two decades older.

Margo was an attractive woman in her sixties with beautiful brunette hair reaching her shoulders. She was medium build and dressed stylishly. Her blue eyes sparkled when she laughed. Margo had been divorced for years. She had one adult son and one adult daughter.

The writing escapade of the group left few secrets. Margo had a rocky relationship with her daughter, but she was quite close to her son.

"Hannah, I need to talk to you about something. Do you want to meet for lunch? I promised you lunch for your birthday anyway. This could kill two birds with one stone," Margo suggested.

"Sure." Hannah laughed. Killing two birds with one stone was a senior friendly phrase. Plus, listening to Margo would be far more interesting than clearing clothes from her bed, Hannah reasoned. "Where did you have in mind?" Hannah asked.

"I was thinking we could go to that deli in midtown. The one that's supposed to have the best soups and salads. I can't remember the name of it but I can see it in my head."

"I know how that goes. I do it all the time. I can remember something one second and in the next second, I've forgotten. I tell you sometimes I don't know half of what I thought I knew."

"Like you always say in our creative writing class, growing old ain't for sissies." Margo chuckled.

Hannah laughed too. "That's 'cause it's not for sissies. I think the name of that restaurant you're talking about is called Jack's Deli or something like that."

"Yep, that's it. Jack's Deli," exclaimed Margo.

"Okay, then I'll see you in about an hour."

♦

Hannah's mind wondered as she arrived to the restaurant. She had thought of eating lunch here but had never gotten around to it. She was glad Margo suggested it.

The quaint restaurant was not crowded. Hannah spotted Margo almost as soon as she walked inside.

Margo beckoned for her as she entered.

Hannah walked to the table and removed her coat.

Before Hannah was seated, Margo blurted, "Oh, Hannah, it's my son. I can't believe what has happened to our relationship!"

Hannah took a deep breath. Was this *Son, bash your mother* year? she thought herself.

"I don't know what happened, it was so sudden. He got remarried not that long ago and his new wife doesn't like me." Margo cried, looking at Hannah. "He wrote me a letter saying he wanted nothing else to do with me. What can I do?"

Just as Hannah opened her mouth to answer, Margo continued.

"It hurt like hell. I thought I could depend on him. I never allowed anything to come between me and him. I tried talking to him but it seems to only make matters worse," Margo complained. "What did I do wrong?" Margo pulled a tissue from her purse and began dabbing at her eyes.

Another example of not knowing half of what you thought you knew," Hannah mumbled under her breath, shaking her head.

"What am I going to do?" wailed Margo.

"I'll tell you what to do. Go to his house. Sit in his front yard, and do like Job."

"Do what like Job?" Margo looked at her friend quizzically.

"You know what Job did. He dressed in sackcloth and ashes. He lamented. You should do the same. Go to your son crying and begging him," Hannah advised.

Margo's head snapped back. Her eyes full of anger. "Are you out of your mind? Why should I beg when I haven't done anything to him?" she retorted.

Hannah saw her stab at humor was lost on Margo. "I was joking, Margo."

"It's not funny. It's like there's a chill that's settled in my bones, Hannah. I realized I was depressed. After several attempts to talk to him, I decided to let him alone. He drew the line. And I'm too old to lose precious moments of happiness over something that I didn't cause."

Hannah understood this was Margo's moment to vent, so she sat quietly and listened, taking Margo's hands in hers. They sat there for several moments holding each other's hands while Margo talked.

"He accused me of gossiping about his siblings. He said I took his generosity for granted and that I acted like he was obligated to do things for me." Margo wiped her eyes.

They sat quietly for a moment drinking iced tea.

A baritone voice evaded their space and conversation. "Excuse me," he said. "I couldn't help but overhear your conversation."

Hannah and Margo both turned, giving their attention to a man seated at a table across from them.

"May I?" he got up from where he was seated. Before they could answer, he had come around and sat at their table. "Believe me, I don't go around listening to other people's private conversations, but I was sitting there and I heard you. You don't know this, but what you're talking about is an answer to my prayer."

"What do you mean?" said Margo, clearing her face with a handkerchief she pulled out of her purse.

"You see, I came in here to get something to eat and clear my head," the man said. "By the way, my name is Andrew. Andrew Norris. I had a terrible fight with my mother. I'm one of five siblings, the middle child. I love my mother with all my heart, but recently resentment has formed and it's overwhelming."

"If you don't mind me asking, how old are you?" Hannah asked.

"Fifty," he replied. "A lot of things changed for me as I matured. My mother and I have always been close, but recently it seems like we've grown apart. There are issues I'd like to discuss with her, but she is so distracted. It's like before I can finish my thoughts, she tells me about my sibling's problems. I'm fed up with that behavior."

"Does your mother live here?" Margo inquired.

"No, in Atlanta. My whole family lives there."

The man was neatly dressed with olive complexion that complimented deep brown eyes, which were sheltered under a pair of pencil thin eyebrows. His beard was neatly trimmed and his long black hair was pulled back in Willie Nelson style.

He was tall, of normal build, very distinguished looking, handsome, poised, and dressed in business attire.

"I'm an executive with Nelson and Nelson. We're a consulting firm. I've been with them for twenty-one years," he shared.

The more Margo and Hannah listened to Andrew's concerns, the more his issues reminded them of their own.

"Can I get you ladies something, maybe a glass of iced tea?"

They both nodded and Andrew called the server over. "Three glasses of sweet tea please." He continued talking after the server left. "My mother has always been special to me. As long as I can remember I have worked to please her and make her proud of me."

Margo and Hannah continued listening as his voice echoed.

"My parents divorced when I was nine. I remember my father was abusive at times. They kept their fights from us as much as possible, but children hear things. Honestly, I was happy when he was no longer in the house. There were nights I heard her crying. I promised to do everything within my power to prevent her from crying."

Hannah stirred her as she listened to Andrew.

"That's the way my son was about me. He was so protective," Margo interrupted. "When I received a letter from him that was inundated with accusations, I couldn't believe what I read. I know when I was overwhelmed with problems about his sister I would talk to him about it. He said I was using him as a dumping field. I had no idea he felt that way." Margo sobbed.

"Are you sure you were not gossiping? "Andrew questioned.

"No, I was venting, not gossiping."

"I never wanted to hurt my mother's feelings," Andrew added. "She sacrificed so much for us. At times, she was both father and mother. She put our needs before hers in every situation."

"Andrew, my son said the same thing. I had no idea he felt that way either," Hannah shared. "It was never my intent to breach their trust by talking to my son about his siblings' issues. I realize now I burdened him with things that were of no concern to him."

"It may not have been your intentions; however, it was still a violation. Innocence and ignorance are both infractions," Andrew said. "I had issues I wanted to talk to my mother about. I needed and I wanted her undivided attention." Andrew paused and then started talking again. "After hearing the both of you, I realize things are not always in black and white; there are hues also. I wanted to talk to her about *my* concerns and she turned the conversations to problems my siblings were having. She never heard me. Over time, I started resenting that. For instance, she was upset a few months ago when my siblings didn't come to her house for a holiday dinner. But family dynamics change. Do parents even see or understand that? Do they see our lives as it changes?"

Hannah looked at Andrew. His question was similar to the one her son had asked her. She understood from listening to Andrew, she would have to allow time to resolve the issues between her and her son.

The three of them talked until Andrew stood and excused himself. "I thank you ladies for letting me join you. You made me realize that we as sons are blessed to have caring mothers. I know now that I should have voiced my objections, instead I kept quiet. My mother is important to me. I love her. I am going to do everything in my power to correct our differences." He leaned in and tenderly embraced each lady.

Tears ran down both their faces as they watched Andrew leave the restaurant. The conversation helped but it also condemned them.

"Andrew really put things in perspective for me," Hannah said.

"I'm so glad we met him," Margo said.

"Maybe we should make a list of the things we do not know, things we believed would never change." Hannah chuckled as she placed her hand on Margo's shoulder.

"I think making a list is a good idea," Margo stated.

They sat and reflected on the conversation with Andrew. They had work to do, fences to mend.

8

Hannah stopped at Goodwill after leaving the restaurant. Searching through other people's recycled items made her feel better. She had gained some valuable insight from listening to Andrew. From now on, if a holiday function was not well attended, she told herself she would not get bent out of shape about it. She would keep in mind that non-attendance did not necessarily mean the absence of love. She would learn to handle the changes in her life.

The day was far spent. It was time to get off the streets, being she was no longer a night driver. She pulled into her driveway, got out of her car, and removed the packages from the back seat.

Unlocking the front door, she entered her house, and went straight to the kitchen. She placed one of her dinners in the oven. Next, Hannah checked her mail. Junk mail only. She proceeded to toss it into the waste basket.

When her dinner was ready, she sat at the table and ate while allowing her mind to replay several events that occurred over the past several days. She thought more about MaryLou's suggestion. Forming a group for seniors was an excellent idea. There were many issues that needed to be addressed.

Hannah spent the next several months researching ways to form an effective group. It kept her mind off her troubled relationship with Alvin.

After several months of hard work and countless conversations with her peers, the senior group was in full swing. The group was made up of twenty members so far, including a retired psychologist, a nurse, and two retired social workers.

The meetings were scheduled for the third Tuesday of each month at eleven o'clock. The library had agreed to let the group meet their monthly. Lunch was served as a part of the process.

♦

Sixty-nine year old member, Curtis Watkins, lead the senior discussion at this week's meeting. Curtis and Hannah had spoken on the phone on a number of occasions. His wife died a few months ago. He seemed to be in control, but Hannah wondered if he was really alright. She understood grief takes time and life is unpredictable.

Curtis talked like a speeding locomotive. "I was married for thirty-nine years when my wife suddenly died. We have one son. I've been thinking, do any of you remember when you became an adult and began putting your plans in motion?" Several of the members in attendance nodded. "Well, when you look at where you are now, would you say you handled life or did life handle you?" Curtis continued, not waiting on a response. "I mean, think about it. There are so many unseen occurrences that we absolutely have no control over. Things like sickness, poor health, failed marriages, divorce, unfaithfulness, bankruptcy and death. When the hand is dealt, no matter what it is, we must play it. We are not equipped for the game change. If we were, we would be God."

Hannah observed several group members nodding in agreement.

Curtis dominated the meeting. Those in attendance seemed to understand his need to vent.

Soon, after he had talked for some time, he relinquished the floor and another member by the name of Roxie Cole took the floor.

"Hello, I'm Roxie Cole," she started. Roxie was a petite woman of about seventy years old, with gray hair she wore up in a bun. Much like MaryLou, Roxie was a stylish dresser.

"I understand your grief," she said, looking at Curtis. My husband was part of a singing group. He was killed on his way to a singing engagement. Imagine my surprise when I received a telephone call from the hospital informing me he had been in an accident and was in critical condition. They wanted my permission to place him on a ventilator. You have no idea the mental anguish when I realized he was already gone and the machine only gave me false hope," Roxie said, trembling. "I hope this group will be able to help me deal with my grief and what happened to my husband. It's hard making it on my own at my age."

Roxie, Curtis, and several of the other members shared their feelings openly. Hannah was pleased with the outcome. At the end of the meeting, everyone pitched in and helped tidy up the meeting room.

Hannah filed her reports and placed them in the cabinets in alphabetical order before leaving for the day.

9

Rachel Banks sat in the doctor's office in her wheelchair. She was oblivious to whatever the doctor was saying. That's because she was so angry. Life wasn't fair.

"There is nothing physically wrong with your legs. I've told you this on many occasions, Ms. Banks. You simply have given up on everything since your husband's death," Doctor James said. "There is nothing you can do to bring your husband back. You have to come to terms with his death." He took her hands in his. "Perhaps you will reconsider my suggestion to seek professional counseling."

Rachel remained quiet and motionless.

"Ms. Banks, if you continue in this manner, your son can have you committed to a mental hospital. He *is* your Power of Attorney," Kathy, her nurse said.

Kathy, a twenty-seven year old registered nurse, had been hired by Rachel's son, Luke Wilson, to take care of his mother. Luke was hard to understand and difficult to work for. Kathy felt he was the kind of son who would hide his mother in an institution. Kathy didn't want that to happen to Rachel.

Since her husband's death, Rachel seemed to have lost her will to live. Kathy did what she could to cheer Rachel up.

Rachel's mind was in another place. She had been married twice and both husbands had died, making her a widow twice. What did it matter if Luke placed her in some institution? She didn't care. Maybe she would save her medication and commit suicide.

"Ms. Banks, do you hear me?" Dr. James said. Unfortunately, Dr. James had seen this type of depression in many of his patients. It concerned him because this woman had so much to live for. She was still in the prime of life, very attractive although she did little if anything about her appearance. Her hair was always styled. That was because Luke had someone from the hair salon do his mother's hair, weekly.

Rachel continued to tune out Dr. James by thinking thoughts of both of her late husbands. Harold, her second husband, was such a patient man. He loved her and her two sons dearly.

Hannah's oldest son's father, David Winston, died when their son was still young. Life had been unfair.

Rachel met David when he and a group of Marines were assigned to the same military base where Rachel's father was stationed. Her father was a corporal in the Army. Her mother was a nurse, and Rachel was a military brat.

She was quickly mesmerized by David. The couple had a whirlwind affair. After a year of courtship, they got married. They were so happy, but Rachel worried about him being a Marine. She did not want him to go into active duty so she convinced him to sever his term with the Corps and join the Merchant Marines.

The irony was a freak accident claimed his life. A defective bomb accidentally went off, striking the oil cruiser that was delivering oil to David's ship, killing every crew member.

David Winston had been dead for three years when Rachel met Harold

Banks one afternoon while walking her son, Seth, in the park.

"Miss...Miss you dropped your child's hat," she heard someone call from behind her.

Rachel turned around and saw the man running towards her with Seth's blue cap in his hand. She waited until he caught up with her.

Many of her so-called White friends frowned at the fact that Seth's father was Black. Harold wasn't bothered about Seth's racial mixture, nor was he turned off by the fact of her involvement with a Black man. A lot of men resented that fact.

When he walked up to her with Seth's cap in his hand, Rachel immediately noticed the man's warm smile as he gave her the baby's cap.

"Thank you," she told him.

"You're welcome. My name is Harold Banks," he told Rachel.

"Hi, Harold. My name is Rachel."

"Do you live in this area? Are you married?" Harold asked boldly. He had to know because he really wanted to get to know this woman. He had seen her walking with the little boy on a few other occasions but never said anything. Today had been his opportunity when he saw the little boy's cap fall to the ground.

"I'm a widow," Rachel answered

"Please, I hope I'm not too forward, but would you care to have a cup of tea with me. There's a diner on the corner." He pointed in the direction of the corner strip mall.

Rachel stood for a moment, speechless. There was something comforting about this man. "Yes," she replied.

After they finished their tea, he walked her back to the park where she'd left her car parked. He helped her put Seth's stroller inside.

"May I call you sometime? Maybe we can have dinner."

♦

Harold and Rachel ended up getting married. After they were married, he insisted he be allowed to adopt Seth as his own son. Both sides of their families approved of their relationship.

Harold was easy to love. He was a gentle man who loved Seth and Rachel. There were many pockets of prejudice and he did not want there to be problems where Seth's inheritance would be concerned.

Rachel thought about Hannah, the woman she'd met in the park. Hannah had asked Rachel if she thought Harold would understand Rachel's desire to die and be with him. Rachel told Hannah that Harold would not be happy with her if she did something like that. As a matter of fact, Harold always made her promise if something ever happened to him that she should go on with her life and live it to the fullest. For the first time since Harold's death, Rachel understood she *did* have something to live for—herself.

Hannah had been right; she had given up after Harold's death. She sat in her apartment in deep thought about the grief that consumed her, and the fact the doctor told her there was no reason she shouldn't be able to walk. Physically, there was nothing wrong with her, mentally, well the grief kept her bound in more ways than one.

She had avoided Luke lately, even refusing to answer his phone calls. It was the only way she could think clearly about the next step she was ready to take in her life. Luke was the kind of person who insisted on control. She loved her son, but at the same time she knew how stubborn he could be when his mind was on a certain thing.

10

The phone rang, dragging Hannah's mind back to the present.

"Hello, Rachel, would you like to go to the park with me today?" It was her friend Kathy.

"Yes, I'd like that. Let me give you my new address. You know I'm living in Senior Villas, the facility Seth manages."

"I didn't know you moved already. You said you were thinking about moving, but you didn't say when or where. What did Luke have to say?"

"You know Luke doesn't approve but it is what it is. Before things got too out of control, I contacted my attorney and revoked Luke's Power of Attorney. He mailed a copy to Luke showing I rescinded his control over my affairs."

"Good for you, Hannah."

"We'll talk about it when we meet at the park," Hannah said.

"Okay, I'll see you soon."

Hannah buttoned her coat and adjusted her scarf as she walked to the park. She missed her walks in the park. She had been on vacation the past week with her daughter, Ruth. They had a great time visiting relatives, but Hannah was glad to be back home.

The air outside was refreshing, a typical autumn day. As she walked along the familiar walking trail, she recognized Rachel at first glance. Rachel was not in a wheelchair and she was alone without a caregiver.

Hannah rushed to her, said hello, and gave Rachel a big hug. "Rachel, it's so good to see you!"

"Hannah, I can't believe it's you." Rachel beamed with joy. "I have been to this park many times, hoping I would run into you again.

"You look good, Rachel. And, oh my gosh, you're not in your wheelchair." Hannah sat next to Rachel while scanning the park. "And where is your caregiver?"

"That's why I've been hoping to run into you again. I want to thank you."

"Thank *me*? Why? For what?"

"When we met, I had allowed grief to cloud my judgement. My doctor kept telling me that my illness and failure to walk was all in my mind. I finally heard what he was saying, but it was only after I met you. You're the one who

76

made me realize I had stopped living after Harold died, and Harold would not want me to be that way. So I prayed about it and I changed my life around."

Hannah was speechless.

"Things are so much better now. I even moved into a senior facility where one of my son's manages."

"That's fantastic; what a blessing," Hannah remarked.

"That's my car parked over there." Rachel pointed to the parking lot where a white P.T. Cruiser was parked.

"You...you're driving, too?" Hannah couldn't believe the remarkable change in Rachel.

"Yep. I had forgotten how much I used to enjoy driving."

"I'm so happy for you, Rachel."

"Thank you. I feel better than I have in a long time."

"Now that you're back to living life again, I'd like to invite you to be part of my Seniors Assistance Group. Your story would encourage many of the group members."

"Sounds like something I might be interested in," Rachel replied. "When do you meet?"

"We meet the second Tuesday starting at eleven o'clock at the Center City Library. A light lunch is provided."

"Okay, I'll try to make the next meeting."

"Let me give you my information. I don't want us to lose contact this time."

Both ladies exchanged information before parting ways.

♦

When Rachel pulled into her parking space, she spotted Luke getting out of his car.

She parked her Cruiser at the same time she met Luke's gaze.

He stopped walking when he saw her and began his onslaught of questions. "When did you decide to drive again? What's gotten into you, Ma? What do you think you're doing? "Where have you been? This is why I'm concerned about you, especially when you start listening to Seth. I'm beginning to wonder if you're safe with him."

Rachel couldn't believe her ears. Luke reminded her of one of those children who have complete control over their parents' lives. Rachel was stunned for a moment. "Luke, I'm of sound mind and capable of taking care of myself. I know you don't think so, but believe me, I'm fine. It's time for me to start living again. Harold is dead; I'm not."

"I should have listened to Megan. She said I should have had you committed when I had the chance. If Seth wasn't in the picture, there would be no problem," Luke complained.

"Your wife doesn't know what she's talking about. Why would she want to have me committed? I'm not crazy!" Rachel fumed.

"What*ever*, Mother."

Rachel glared at her son, detecting anger in his eyes as he got in his car. She stood quiet, watching him drive away. Upset, Rachel sat in her car after he left, trying to clear her head before facing Seth.

She was startled when Seth knocked on her window. "Mama, what are you doing sitting out here? I've been waiting for you. It's dinner time."

For a moment, she saw Seth's father standing before her, handsome and charismatic.

Rachel felt her car door open, bringing her back to the moment. "Mama, is everything alright?" Seth asked again.

"I'm good, Seth. Everything's fine. I was out here talking to your brother," she explained as Rachel exited the car and followed her son into the facility.

"What did he say? You look like you're upset about something."

"You know how your brother can be."

"He objects to you living here, doesn't he?"

"He wants the best for me just like you."

"I don't care. He has no right to be angry with you. He stormed into my office a few weeks ago, accusing me of alienating your affections," Seth said. "I had to put him in his place. He can come up with some of the most asinine stuff. He's my brother and I love him, but he can work my nerves."

Rachel chuckled but did not say anything else about it. They walked into the almost deserted lobby. Many of the residents were engaged in other activities in other areas of the large facility.

The Senior Villas sat on a ninety-acre lot. It was equipped with a health club, library, a two-hundred seat theater, dining room, game room, chapel, beauty salon and a barbershop.

"Seth, don't let Luke get you all upset. You know how he is."

"Yeah, I know, but I don't know what happened between me and him. When we were growing up, we had the best relationship ever. It was like he was my best friend, although I was his big brother. I was the one who looked out for him." They walked to a row of chairs and were seated.

You were always Luke's protector."

"That's because you taught us to always look out for one another. I remember when we were kids, he would jump into my bed whenever he heard the slightest noise." Seth laughed. "I was his protector all right. Then when we became teenagers, things started changing. There was the name calling by a few of his friends, but never where you or father could overhear."

"Did Luke object when his friends called you ugly names?"

"He did, but it didn't stop them from bullying me."

Rachel wondered if Seth being African-American had perhaps secretly been an issue with Harold. She wondered if he had ever had negative conversations with their son.

"Daddy loved me. He often mentioned my birth father. He said what an honorable man he must have been because you loved him so much."

Hannah smiled. Seth had just answered her question.

11

Rachel and Seth talked while they had dinner. Rachel shared the story with Seth about his father, David.

"Your father swept me off my feet."

Seth chuckled at seeing his mother's face beam with joy as she spoke.

"Yes, David Winston mesmerized me the day he walked into the VFW Club. He literally took my breath away. He was handsome as could be. You inherited every one of his features." She smiled and looked proudly at Seth.

"Your father looked like a Greek God to me, with flawless sandy brown complexion and piercing dark eyes. His features reflected his strong African-American heritage. His thick, curly hair lay in layers close to the side of his head. When I touched his face, it felt like soft velvet. Ours was a whirlwind affair.

My parents voiced concern at first. They had endured racial issues because my mother was white and your grandfather was black."

Seth listened as his mother continued. He'd heard the story before but he never tired of her telling it.

"When they realized how much we loved each other, they gave us their blessings. Your father's family, on the other hand, objected."

"Why? Because you were an interracial couple?" remarked Seth.

"Yes, mostly. You see, your grandfather was a powerful business tycoon. He hated the idea that your father was going to marry a white woman. David did not share your grandfather's views about race or the business world.

His father warned David if he married me he was going to disown him and he would no longer consider him as his son.

David married me in spite of his father's objections and threats. David's father kept his promise and disowned David. I'm surprised prejudice manifested itself in your brother though," Rachel said.

"Luke wasn't bothered by my heritage. At least, I don't think he was. Luke felt more threatened by my popularity. I don't think he ever forgave me for dating Clara Mae Montgomery, but I couldn't help it if she chose me instead of him. Plus, I didn't know he liked her until after me and her got together. He even told me I stole your love from him, and stole his father's love from him," Seth said.

Rachel's eyes filled with tears at hearing this. There were issues between Luke and Seth, but Rachel quickly pushed the unpleasant thoughts from her mind.

Seth held on to his mother's every word. In the past, his mother couldn't talk to him about his father without her eyes filling with tears. Today was different. His mother glowed while talking about his father and the love they had for one another.

"David loved the water, the open sea. He joined the Marine Corps and later the Merchant Marines." Rachel's voice lowered and her head dropped. "The very sea he loved so much claimed him."

Seth looked up when one of the staff members approached.

"Excuse me, Mr. Winston, you're needed in the front office," said the young woman. "Your appointment is here."

Hearing the woman call her son's name reminded Rachel of Seth's decision to take his father's sir name of Winston instead of Harold's name of Banks. He said though Harold adopted him, he still felt an obligation to carry on his father's lineage.

"Mother, I've got to go. I'll walk you to your flat."

They left the dining room, walked from the vestibule, pass the lounge area, until they arrived at the corridor leading to Rachel's flat.

"I'll stop by later, Ma," Seth said, leaning in and kissing Rachel on the cheek.

Rachel noticed a very distinguished gentleman sitting in the common area. He smiled. Rachel blushed.

"Mom, I saw that." Seth embraced his mother playfully. "If you care to know, his name is August Russell. He's new here. He just relocated from New York. He's retired and a widower. He has a daughter and two grandchildren who live in the city. I guess that may be why he moved to Massy," Seth shared.

Rachel smiled when she recalled Hannah's routine. She already knew he wasn't married. Now all she needed to find out was how old he was and his phone number.

12

Sixty-four year old widower August Russell was young in spirit and appearance. He was one of the new residents at Senior Villas. August was looking forward to what he hoped would be a positive move for him.

August, a retired Baptist preacher, was faithfully committed to his church. Though he was retired, he still served the Lord in whatever ministerial capacity he could. In his heyday, August had been blessed with a thriving ministry, but after Debra's death, he resigned from his pastoral role. His daughter had been trying to convince him to move to Massy so he could be closer to her and his grandchildren. At first, August balked at the idea. He wanted to remain in New York near his friends and his church. But he was also lonely, very lonely, without the love of his life. He began to entertain the idea of moving. The house was too big for just one person. He had no pets to keep his mind occupied. His one true desire was to render service in ministry, but not as the pastor of a church again. He had served as pastor in Rome for twenty-four years. Debra loved their church family. So did he, but it was time to move forward. Time for a change.

The deaths of his beloved Debra, his baby daughter, and now his son-in-law drew him closer to the Lord. He reminded himself that all have a cross to carry. It was difficult at times not to question the will of God. He found courage to keep moving forward by reading the Bible. He particularly liked the story of the life of Job.

As he continued in thought about the move, he thought of Debra. She would want him to find happiness. They had discussed that aspect of life on many occasions, promising each other they would not spend the rest of their lives forever grieving if one of them died.

August made the decision to move. He wanted to be near his family, his grandchildren, and start a new life. Being close to his only daughter and his grandchildren would do him good. He loved them dearly. He also wanted to be in Massy for Karen's sake after her husband was killed.

Karen's husband, Walter, died in a head-on collision with a drunk driver. She was devastated. After his death, she initially thought about moving from Massy, Ohio back to Rome, New York. It was her thoughts that perhaps going back to New York might help her adjust better to life without Walter. It was hard passing the scene of where the accident happened. It was on the same route Walter used to take to travel to work. Karen had to avoid that area altogether if she planned to move on through her grief.

Karen met Walter Richmond when she attended college in Massy. Massy was his hometown. He lived on campus at the small private institution. It was love at first sight when Karen first laid eyes on him. She was an out-of-state student from Rome, New York.

After they graduated from college, they found lucrative jobs in New York and so they relocated there. They made successful lives for themselves, got married, settled down, and had the twins.

After his death, Karen moved back to Massy where Walter's family still lived.

Karen believed it would be good for her and the kids. It would also be good for Walter's mother who had a mental breakdown after Walter died. Having her grandchildren around helped her mother-in-law's recovery.

August understood his daughter's decision to move to Massy permanently. Of course, she wanted him to move to Massy, too. It took some praying, prodding and heavy persuasion, but August finally gave in, especially after he visited Massy to see his daughter and grandkids. He saw Massy was a nice, safe, and quiet small town.

August was also concerned with his daughter's state of mind since Walter's death. When he talked to her on the phone or chatted with her on facetime, Karen appeared happy and care free. Walter saw through her act. He felt she was pretending to be fine but he didn't think she was. Her faith and trust in God has been surely shaken. August sensed resentment and anger from her when he talked of God's will in their life.

13

Karen sat on the sofa sipping a glass of wine and looking at her wedding pictures. Seeing the beautiful memories of her and Walter, and remembering the years of bliss they shared, brought tears to her eyes until they overflowed and cascaded down her red cheeks. The pain of her loss was mind boggling. A bout of anger came out of nowhere, followed by a sick feeling that engulfed Karen. Hiding her face in her hands, she tried, though unsuccessful, to control her heaving sobs. She was so mad at God.

Rather than allow herself to keep sinking further into depression, she called her father. She was thankful he lived in Massy now. He had managed somehow to secure a prime spot at Senior Villas, one of the top residents in the city for people 55 and up. It was known to have an extensive waiting list. But God showed favor toward August.

After talking to August, Karen ended the call in a much better frame of mind. Her daddy always had that calming effect on her. Karen smiled at the thought of how loving, compassionate and gentle he was. She remembered how he would do her mother the same way. When her mother was upset about something or had a rough day or ran into a problem she couldn't handle, August was right there with words of encouragement and love. He was not a man who was quick to anger; just the opposite. August had a soothing spirit about himself. He was a great listener and a godly counsel.

♦

Senior Villas was made up of 77 flat-level bungalow units. No worries about stairs or failing elevators. August's spacious two-bedroom unit was equipped with everything he desired.

Senior Villas offered a common area where residents could gather, socialize, eat meals and be entertained.

August stood in the bathroom mirror and took inventory of himself. He was still a virile, handsome man. Women seemed to adore him. He was generous, polite and if he had to admit; charming.

93

A widower, his wife of almost forty years, Debra, passed away four years ago. August missed her terribly. She had been the love of his life. He met and married Debra when they were both nineteen years old. They had two children. Their youngest child, Monica, unfortunately died in childbirth. His daughter, Karen, had two children of her own, twins named Samuel and Samella. They visited him often. Family involvement was encouraged at Senior Villas.

Concerned about his well-being, Karen worried about August being alone. It was one of the reasons she was glad and somewhat relieved when August told her he was moving out of the huge empty house he once shared with his wife and daughter, and relocating to Massy, Ohio. He told her he found a nice *55 and older* complex called Senior Villas. He would be around other seniors and there was a medical staff on sight.

Karen couldn't have been happier. She had been trying to convince her father to put the house up for sale and come there, but it was like pulling teeth.

He wouldn't do it. Thank God her father relented and made the move.

14

Rachel showered, dressed, and checked her appearance before leaving her flat. It was the second Tuesday of the month, the day for the senior's group meeting Hannah started. Rachel gave Hannah her word she would attend. Rachel was looking forward to getting out, exploring life again, and seeing how other seniors lived, especially those who were widows like her.

She wanted to look her best in case the gentleman who gave her such an inviting smile the other day would be there. From what she'd already learned about him from Seth, he was a widower too who had just moved into Senior Villas.

On her way outside to the parking lot, she passed by the game room. She stopped at the door to the game room when she saw him seated at a table playing cards with four other men. She tried not to look too conspicuous but it was hard. She placed one hand over her chest, stopped in her tracks, when she saw him look up and then get up from the card table and come towards her.

"Excuse me," he said when he approached her. Rachel was about to walk off.

"Yes?" Rachel looked at him and remarked, nervous because she hadn't talked to anyone of the opposite sex since Harold's death.

"I'm new here. I saw you the other day but you were with the director so I didn't think it was the right time to introduce myself. My name is August Russell."

"Hi, nice to meet you, August."

"I don't mean to be forward but I've seen you around Senior Villas on several occasions. I hoped I would get the chance to properly introduce myself."

Rachel turned crimson, smiled, and then cautiously extended her hand towards his. "My name is Rachel Banks. I'm new to Senior Villas too. I moved in two weeks ago."

"Is that so? Well, maybe we can show each other around the Villas. There's so much to explore. I can see why this is the number one place for seniors to live. It's first class."

"Yes, it is. The director is my son, so I'm familiar with where everything is. I can show you around if you'd like," Rachel casually offered.

"Oh, so Seth Winston is your son, huh?"

"Yes."

"Umm, is that right? Well, maybe I should talk to him to see if he can put in a good word to you on my behalf." He flashed a charming smile her way.

Rachel returned his smile with one of her own.

"Should we start our tour around the Villas with dinner this evening?" He let out the breath he was holding.

"I would be delighted to dine with you this evening," Rachel answered.

"Okay, well dinner it is. Shall we meet in the dining room and at what time?"

"Yes, meet me in the dining room, but I have an outside appointment with a friend, but I should be finished in time to meet you for dinner. If I had your phone number I could call you when I was finished with my meeting," Rachel suggested, taking Hannah's advice to be more forward.

"That's a good idea. Here you go." August reached into his pant pocket, pulled out his wallet, opened it, and removed a business card and handed it to Rachel.

Rachel smiled as she drove to Hannah's meeting. It was nice having someone of the opposite sex interested in her. There were so many questions going on in her mind, what did she expect from life at age sixty-three and twice widowed.

She wished she was more like Hannah. Hannah often said, *"Life is not a dress rehearsal. It will not come again so if a brass ring presents itself, catch it."*

Rachel agreed with Hannah. Life was too short to waste a moment. That rang even truer after having recently attended the funeral of, not one, but two friends in two weeks. One died from complications of a stroke, the other from a heart attack. Life could be challenging enough even without the numerous negative issues that often accompanied aging.

Rachel pulled into a parking space. Before exiting the car, she checked her appearance one more time. Walking toward the library, she stopped briefly, pressed the key FOB to lock the car, and then entered the building.

Rachel entered the meeting room. There were at least ten or fifteen people gathered at tables, eating and chatting. Hannah greeted her and led her to her table while briefly introducing her to those she passed by.

The floor opened for members to talk about whatever was on their minds. Of course, Curtis Watkins was the first one to step up. When he came to the podium, Hannah was shocked, to say the least, at the change in his appearance. He actually had on something other than his usual signature coveralls. He looked rather handsome in a pair of upscale blue jeans and a nice light blue shirt. She wondered what or who was responsible for such a change in Curtis.

Curtis began his conversation by saying, "Hannah, tell the group when you plan to write a book about the sexual behaviors of people over seventy.

100

You write about love and romance, but I'd like to read one of your books specifically geared toward that subject."

"I'm working on it." Hannah chuckled. Those in the room laughed along with her.

"I'm serious," Curtis said.

"Curtis, why don't you tell us what brought about your change of attire. I mean, I like your coveralls, but this is a different look for you. You look so handsome. I might consider giving you a run for your money," Hannah teased.

Curtis shook his head and laughed. "I wanted y'all to see that I have other clothes," he said and laughed. "I just particularly like coveralls. Always have since I was a youngster."

Hannah also noticed his laugh was softer and he appeared more open. She was glad to see the positive change in Curtis.

Mattie Washington, another member of the seniors' group, was a seventy-four year old, pleasingly plump senior, with gorgeous gray hair. She was concerned with her relationship with her only son, Calvin, who was forty-five. He had met a woman and was spending a lot of time with her and Mattie felt threatened.

"I don't like the woman he's seeing. She's trying to separate me and my son. She makes no secret she doesn't like me, and the feeling is mutual," Mattie said.

Nora Works, age sixty-nine, reminded Mattie that she said the same thing about any woman Calvin was involved with.

"That is *not* true. I have to look out for my Calvin. You wouldn't understand, Nora, because you do not have children," Mattie snapped.

"'I may not have children but it doesn't take rocket science to know that adult children have to live their own lives," Nora shot back.

"I have three sons myself," said one of the other seniors. "And Nora is right, Mattie. You have to let them make their own mistakes, and make their own choices. I learned a long time ago to respect their choices of lady friends. If I don't particularly like one of them I keep that opinion to myself."

"Yes, I know, but Calvin is all I have," Mattie said, sounding like she was on the verge of tears. "Calvin's father left me for a younger woman. You know men can do that. Society judges women by a different standard. We have to hide what we feel and pretend we're not effected by such behavior."

"That's why you have to find ways to keep yourself involved and active, Mattie," Hannah added. "Do not allow Calvin to become your crutch. That goes for each one of you who may be dealing with similar issues. Live your own life. We only get this one shot. And on another note, ladies you do not have to be involved with a man in order to be fulfilled."

"Hmmm, who told you that crap?" Mattie blurted out.

"Mattie, Hannah's right," said another one of the women. "I know it hurts when you see your ex out with her, like they're all happy and in love, but you have to push pass it. Like Hannah said, you don't need him or any man for happiness and fulfillment."

"Yes, I know, but I just never thought that something like this could happen to us. I thought he was happy with me, with our relationship. We were married for thirty years. I gave him the best years of my life."

Rachel listened in awe at the deep and open discussions of the group. She was impressed by it and was learning a lot.

"My husband became involved with a younger woman, too so I know how you feel, Mattie. It hurt, it hurt really bad, but I told myself I had to go on with my life. I wasn't going to jump off the bridge because he was unfaithful," Nora said. "Anyway, his young thang left him a year later for a younger man. Karma is something else," Nora said with a huge smile showing her absolute delight.

"Did he want to come back home after she dumped him?" Rachel spoke up and asked.

"Yes, he tried and tried to get me to take him back. And to be honest, I thought about it and almost said yes. Then I thought what if some other younger woman notices him. Would he do the same thing again? I wasn't going to take that chance so I told him to hit the road jack and don't you come back no more." She laughed, and so did some of the other members.

All eyes were focused on Nora. Even Curtis was quiet.

"I did meet this fellow name Hank. He's five years younger than me, so I guess I'm doing the same thing my ex- did when it comes to seeing someone younger. But the difference is I told Hank we could be friends only. I let him know I didn't want to get involved with anyone right now," Nora said.

"You should give him a chance. Just because one man was unfaithful, doesn't mean they all are," Curtis said.

Minnie Jones was fifty-five. She had remained quiet during most of the meeting, but this particular topic of discussion she wanted to give her opinion.

"I've been sitting here listening to the discussion. I don't know about any of you all, but aging is difficult for me. My husband died last year and left me financially set. Because of that, I am extremely careful who I allow into my life. People can be so conniving these days. I'm going to use some of my money to invest in opening a fortune teller's business. I've always been clairvoyant."

"Really. Tell me, do you ever see your dead husband?" Curtis asked.

"Yes, I do, actually. That is one of the main reasons I'm studying about extrasensory perception. I've been talking to different psychics so I can learn everything there is about it."

Keeping a set time frame was one of Hannah's goals. "We've had quite an entertaining meeting today," she said after Nora finished talking. "But it's time for us to part. The meeting is adjourned. I look forward to seeing you all at next month's meeting."

Rachel and Hannah walked outside and stopped to chat.

"Did you enjoy the meeting?"

"Yes, I did. It was fun and informative. I learned a lot. I'm so glad you invited me."

"And I'm glad you came," Hannah remarked.

"Hannah, do you have a few minutes? I'd like to talk to you about something."

"Sure, what's going on?"

"Well, one of the residents at my complex invited me to join him in the dining room this evening for dinner."

"Ooohhhhh, that's great. What did you say?"

"I accepted but I'm so nervous."

Hannah suppressed a smile. "Listen, being nervous is common. It's been a long time since you've talked to a man. It can be scary, but you're starting to live your life again, Rachel. You deserve this. All you have to do is stay in the moment. Don't worry about tomorrow or yesterday."

"But there are so many do's and don'ts running through my mind. And the truth is I don't know if I want to be locked in to anyone or in a relationship. I ran across this article the other day where it said human beings have a prey-predator mentality at a certain age. Hannah, do you think a more open relationship is possible as we mature or do we have to feel possessed, or do we want to be possessed? "

"Ummm, I'll have to think about that one. But you know that's an interesting topic. We need to discuss it at next month's meetup I've learned from listening and talking to other seniors how different aging is for each of us. For me, personally, marriage is not as important as having an open friendship."

"I don't have it all figured out yet. I guess in time I'll know where the rest of my life is headed, but I do want to thank you for listening and sharing your thoughts," Rachel said.

"Anytime," said Hannah.

The two women said their goodbyes and got into their respective vehicles.

♦

Hannah arrived home, unlocked the door, went inside, and placed her keys on the key rack. It had been a long day. She sat at her kitchen table. The kitchen was Hannah's favorite room in her home.

The senior meetings seemed to be beneficial to those who participated. At each meeting, more seniors showed up. That made Hannah glad she had started the group.

She switched her thoughts to her son. She had an idea about the burr that was under her son's saddle. The more she thought about him and his feelings, the more she began to understand that sometimes we are so busy waiting on our time to talk that we fail to hear or listen to the person who is talking to us. That's what she felt like she had been doing when it came to Alvin. Before he finished sharing his concerns, Hannah would jump in with a conversation about *her* concerns, which usually were about one of her other children's problems. When he decided to contact her again, she would listen attentively to his every word.

Every time the phone rang, Hannah hoped it was Alvin. She was anxious to begin repairing their relationship.

15

"Rachel, you seemed a little withdrawn today. I know this was just your second meeting but I hope you're finding it enjoyable. What did you think of the session?" Hannah asked while the ladies talked on the phone.

"I told you I enjoyed it. I could relate to a lot of what was discussed today, especially when the discussion was opened up about seniors and the relationship we have with our children. Seth and I have a good relationship, but I'm at odds with Luke. Luke and I had an awful argument a few days ago. He said I need to rethink my living situation. He doesn't want me living at Senior Villas."

"Our children can be so controlling, especially when we get into our golden years."

"Yes, that's true. You know, Hannah, when my husband died, it took a lot out of me. I felt guilty because Seth was without a father. I know it wasn't my fault but I still blamed myself. When I met and married Harold three years later, I was happy again, He was a decent and kind man. He treated Seth like his own flesh and blood. I was so grateful that Seth had a father, even though he wasn't his biological dad. All I could think about was Seth's welfare. I didn't see it then, but looking back I see it clearly now. You see, I couldn't for the life of me let go of my memories of David. When Harold told me he wanted a child with me, I did not want to have one. I wanted Seth to have Harold to himself. I was living with Harold but still in love with my dead husband." Rachel smiled as she remembered the patience of her second husband. "I don't know why it was so difficult to let David's memory rest."

Hannah didn't say anything, she listened quietly.

"Anyway, enough about my past. I'm sure you have a ton of other stuff to do. I'm going to take a nap. Thank you so much for listening to me, Hannah. You're a blessing."

"Anytime you want to talk, I'm here to listen. I'll talk to you later."

Hannah sat at the desk for a while after Rachel hung up. It had been another long but productive day. She was actually looking forward to dinner and a bit of happy talk. She went through some mail she hadn't had a chance to open. There was an envelope addressed to her with the word URGENT written on it. There was no return address on it.

"Ummm, who could this be from?" She opened the envelope and removed the letter inside.

Hannah, we haven't met yet but my name is Alice Mays. I was at the senior's meeting but I was too embarrassed to speak out. I need help. I am being abused by my landlord. I have no family and nowhere else to go. A neighbor told me about your group. She told me that you help seniors with various problems. I hope you can help me. I feel so foolish not being able to handle my own affairs. I want to move out but my landlord has my personal information and my Social Security check goes to him as payee. That's a whole other concern—I no longer want him to get my monthly benefits. There are three other seniors who live here. He takes all of their money too."

The letter was signed and had a phone number. Hannah called the number. "Hello, is this Alice Mays?"

"Yes, this is Alice," came a timid voice.

"Alice, this is Hannah. I just read your letter. I want you to know I'm going to do everything I can to help you. I'm going to make a referral to Social Services concerning your situation. I'm also contacting the Aging Commission. You should hear something from both agencies in the next few days. And don't worry, Alice, your confidentiality will be protected until the matter is resolved," Hannah assured.

"Thank you so much," Alice said.

No sooner did she finish talking to Alice, her phone rang again. She saw it was Alvin.

"Hello," he said.

Hannah talked to him briefly. It was a relatively good conversation. By the time they ended the call, her spirits were lifted. Him calling her was a positive sign. She hummed a happy tune as she thought about her son and how much she loved him.

16

"We're going to have dinner with your grandfather this evening," Karen told her twelve year old twins after picking one of them up from soccer and the other from gymnastics practice.

"Mama, Granddaddy is so cool. He knows the answer to almost everything," Samuel said and Samella laughed out loud.

Karen was glad her kids had a good relationship with their grandfather. He adored them and they loved him. She couldn't be more grateful of his move to Massy.

The same as her friends wanted her to allow someone into her life, Karen wanted her father to find a companion. She knew he missed her mother because she missed her mother too, and she ached for Walter.

"Okay, you two. I'll wait out here. You all go get your granddaddy," she said after parking a few cars away from August's bungalow.

"Okay, Mommy," Samella said. "Come on, Samuel," she ordered her twin.

Moments later, Karen watched as the twins approached their grandfather's door. She watched as the door opened and they went inside. Ten minutes later, she saw them coming out of his bungalow. She watched as he locked the door then focused his attention on the twins. It made her heart swell with joy seeing the expression of love shared between the three most important people in her life.

She got out of her car as she saw them walking toward the sidewalk. Walking up to him, she embraced her father. "Hi, Daddy. Don't you look handsome," she laughed.

"You look beautiful yourself," he said, leaning and kissing his daughter on her forehead. They walked the short walk to the other side of the main building which housed the dining room among a number of other rooms and amenities for the residents.

"I invited one of the other residents to join us for dinner. I hope you don't mind. Her name is Rachel. She's the director's mother. And he might join us as well, but I'm not sure just yet."

"Uh, I guess that's okay. I mean, it's not like the dining room is a private area. I'm just glad you like living here and that you're meeting people. This is really a nice place. There's so much for you to do, too."

"Yeah, there is. It's always something going on around here. That's what I like about it. I'm glad I was able to secure a spot here. Come on, let's get a table."

The twins chose a table near the vast picture window showcasing the perfectly manicured landscape surrounding Senior Villas.

Shortly after being seated, August excused himself. "I'll be right back. I'm going to go see if I see Rachel. I want her to know where we're sitting."

"Okay, Daddy." Rachel smiled, happy to see her father in such a bright mood, especially when talking about someone of the opposite sex.

She turned around when one of the twins said, "Ma, can we go to the game room?"

"No, Samuel. You can't be running around this place like you're one of the residents. And it's dinner time anyway. You'll get a chance to go to the game

116

room some other time with your grandpa."

Someone approached their table and spoke to Karen and the twins. Karen liked how friendly everyone appeared to be. She talked to the woman a few minutes until the lady excused herself and walked away.

Karen's breath caught in her throat when she saw the man standing next to her father inside the dining room entrance. A sophisticated looking petite woman stood between them as the two men chatted.

Karen couldn't take her eyes off the man. She was struck by male grace and power unlike anything she had experienced since meeting and falling in love with Walter. What was happening? She struggled to maintain her composure.

She continued studying the man, noticing his broad shoulders and how the crisp white dress shirt hugged his muscles and chest, accentuating the long slim lines of his body. His curly, sandy-colored hair touched his shoulders.

117

She watched him then turned away quickly when she saw her father, the woman, and the handsome stranger coming toward their table.

"Karen," her father said, pulling out a chair for his guest, "I want you to meet Rachel Banks."

Karen noticed the man who was with her father had gone in the opposite direction and was talking to some of the residents at the other tables.

The woman sat in the chair and August sat in the chair next to her.

Karen extended her hand. "Hi, Rachel. It's nice to meet you. Introduce yourself," she turned and said to the twins.

The twins each politely told Rachel their names.

The servers brought salads and baskets of fresh buttered rolls. Tea and water were already on the tables.

Rachel and Karen talked easily, something that made August feel at ease. He wanted the chance to get to know Rachel, but he also wanted whoever he met to get a stamp of approval from his daughter. Not that he needed Karen's approval, but he wanted her to know he would always love her mother, but he was also a lonely man.

Seth appeared at the table just as the servers were beginning to serve dinner.

"Karen, twins, meet Seth Winston. Seth is the very capable director of Senor Villas."

"And my adorable son," added Rachel proudly.

Her father's voice broke Karen's trance. Seth could easily have passed for a model for a fashion advertisement or better yet, she smiled at the thought, a strong, striking Viking returning from sea. His hazel eyes were warm and inviting; they moved over her with undisguised interest. His face featured a closely shaved beard which emphasized his chiseled cheekbones and his strong African American features. His bronze complexion appeared flawless and his plump lips made her imagine how they would feel pressed against hers. What had come over her?

Seth extended his hand, taking her hand in his. "Hi, Karen. It's nice to meet you. Your father has been raving about you. I can see why."

Karen sat speechless, aware of the sensations roaming her body as a result of him holding her hand.

August interrupted the exchange. "I'm glad you were able to sit and have dinner with us this evening, Seth. I know you're quite the busy man around here."

"You do an outstanding job," Karen said, shyly.

"I'm so proud of him," added Rachel, glancing at her son with a huge smile plastered on her face.

Seth sat facing Karen, an instant attraction to her took him by surprise.

The conversation at the table during dinner remained interesting and the deep timbre of Seth's voice resonated within Karen.

At one point, their eyes locked and an electric current ran the length of his body. *What the hell was that?*

One of the delights of the facility was the movie after dinner. An actual movie theatre was housed inside the structure that served hot buttered popcorn, movie candy, sodas, and the works.

After dinner, the twins were delighted they would see a movie. They entered the theatre room. Seth excused himself, extending his apologies for having to return to his office to complete the evening paperwork and go home for the night.

"It was nice meeting you, Karen. And it was nice to meet you too, Samuel and Samella. The next time you come, make sure your grandpa shows you around this place. There's a lot to see," he said. "Goodnight, August."

"Goodnight, Seth."

"Goodnight, Ma," Seth said, and kissed and hugged his mother before walking away.

During the movie, Karen noticed her father was enamored with Seth's mother. They giggled and shared popcorn during the movie.

Walking her and the twins to her car after the movie ended, August took the opportunity to talk to his daughter while the twins laughed and talked to each other about how their grandpa acted different around the woman he invited to dinner.

"So what do you think about Rachel? I know you two didn't have a chance to really talk or get to know each other, but what was your first impression?"

"She's pretty and she seems nice. A little quiet. She reminds me of Momma in a way. You like her?" Karen boldly asked.

"I do," August replied easily. "This was our first time having dinner together. I just met her a few days ago. She lives in the flats on the other side of the main building," August chirped.

"What do you know about Seth?" Karen asked, trying to be subtle.

August opened the driver's door for his daughter after she pressed the key FOB to unlock it. Waiting on her to get in the car, he glanced over at the twins who were fussing about who was going to sit in the front seat.

"So you're just as enamored by Seth as I am about his mother." His eyebrows raised and both August and Karen chuckled after his comment. Without verbally replying, Karen started the car.

August then closed the door and stepped back from the car.

"Nite, Daddy. Love you."

"Nite, Princess. See you later Samella and Samuel. I love you. Samuel, remember what we talked about. Watch out for your mother and sister."

"I will, Granddaddy."

August turned and walked away. Entering his bungalow, he felt a surge of energy race through his body. He was alive. Fully alive. He hadn't felt this way in years. The reason? None other than— Rachel Banks.

17

It had been days since Rachel heard from Luke. She was concerned. It pushed Rachel to recall the emotional damage she inflicted on her son when he was a child and needed her affection the most. Time had shown her she needed to fix things between them. It was difficult to admit she could not allow her child to embrace her and that she actually avoided him.

When he was ten years old, Luke asked Rachel why she didn't love him or his father. "You don't love anyone but Seth," he screamed at her. Why were these hurtful memories of the past haunting her now? Why? She was having problems sleeping, and the night before she had declined a movie date with August. For some reason, she couldn't concentrate. She was riddled with guilt.

The voice in her head tormented her. *You couldn't love Luke because his birth robbed Seth of a father. You robbed him of a father.* Tears streamed down her face.

"Honey, I'll be safe, don't worry so much," she heard David's voice, saw his face. She'd cried, screamed, pleaded but to no avail. How could she have known her beloved would die in a freak accident? Had God punished her by taking David? So many thoughts raced through her mind.

When she married Harold she didn't plan on having more children. She wanted Seth to have Harold to himself, but then she got pregnant with Luke, Harold's first child. Harold spent so much time with Luke until Rachel resented her own baby.

Harold, being such a compassionate man, must have noticed her struggle because he suggested Rachel seek professional help. He sat in on some of the therapy sessions at her request.

The emotional stumbling block between Rachel and Luke as he grew up continued to grow and loom over them until it was like a giant boulder between them now. Rachel buried her head in her hands and sobbed. What must she do? Maybe she needed to seek professional help like she did all those years ago. At the next senior's group meeting, Rachel decided she would ask some of the members if they knew of a good counselor or psychologist she could talk to.

Rachel arrived to the monthly senior's meeting. No sooner than she had taken a seat and began talking to some of the other attendees, her eyes connected with a gray-haired gentleman who looked awfully familiar. Could it be who she thought? Surely not. It had been years since she'd seen Dr. Brandon Mickens, but turns out it was him, all these years later. Now a seasoned senior, was the doctor who had counseled her years ago when Luke was a child! He came to the meeting at the invitation of one of the other members. He was there to talk about the need for seniors to seek counseling when they needed help with life's problems and situations.

Rachel and Dr. Mickens reunited after the end of the monthly meeting.

"Hello, Rachel. It's good to see you. You haven't changed a bit," he said, smiling. "I recognized your face the moment you entered the meeting. I didn't remember your name of course.

When everyone introduced themselves, and I heard you state your name, I knew it was you. Imagine my surprise. How many years has it been?"

Rachel thought for a moment. "Too many to remember. About forty."

"My how quickly time flies. Did you enjoy my session?" the doctor asked.

"Yes, I was impressed with your input. You're still as sharp as a tack," she said, smiling.

"Working with groups like this keeps me involved. I'm retired, but I still keep myself involved and active. How are you, Rachel?"

"I'm good, but I'm glad our paths crossed again. I trusted you from the first time we met. You made me feel at ease, like I could talk to you about my problems. Well, I know you said you're retired now, but I really need someone to talk to." She teared up.

"Yes, I'm retired, but I still counsel people from time to time. I'd be glad to sit down and talk. As a matter of fact, I'm free for the remainder of the afternoon. If you want to, there's a small restaurant on the Boardwalk called Imagine. We can go there, have a bite to eat and you can tell me what's on your mind. How about that?"

"That sounds perfect."

♦

With their lunch out of the way, Rachel and Dr. Mickens began talking.

"You falsified papers that released your husband from one branch of service to another. You're blaming yourself that he was killed in a setting that you thought was safe."

"You remember my story after all these years? I couldn't bring myself to admit what I'd done," she cried. "I felt such guilt, as if I had killed him myself. If only I hadn't helped him switch from one branch of the military to the next, then maybe he would be alive today."

Dr. Mickens reached across the table and held Rachel's hands in his. "I warned you all those years ago about the damage resentment could cause. That resentment settled onto your son," he explained.

Rachel nodded. "I remember I couldn't stand to kiss or love on my own son." Rachel buried her face in her hands, struggling to control her emotions.

Dr. Mickens got up from where he sat and scooted his chair next to hers. "Listen, Rachel, understand that you have no power to take or give life—that's God's work." He gently lifted her face from her hands. "Whatever you did back then, you did it because you thought you were protecting your husband. We cannot alter fate. Do you know why you resented your son?"

Rachel looked at the doctor teary-eyed, waiting on his answer.

"Because you never really took the time you needed to grieve for your son's father. Sure, I remember talking to you all of those years ago, but from seeing you today and listening to you, you're still wrestling with your past. You allowed your feelings of guilt to spill over and into your baby boy's life," the doctor explained.

Rachel drew a tissue from her jacket pocket and dabbed at her eyes.

"As humans, we like to control things. When we let go and trust a higher power, when we let go and let God, we find peace." The doctor nodded.

129

"You've made peace with yourself. Now make peace with your son. Set aside your pride. Face him and ask his forgiveness," he stressed. "Do not attempt to justify your past behavior."

"Luke is distant. He always seems angry. Every time I see him I feel condemned. I think my feelings of guilt might also be what's getting in the way of me having a relationship again."

"Rachel, it's time for you to let go of the past. You've got to learn how to let sleeping dogs stay asleep."

"I know you're right, Dr. Mickens, but it's just so hard."

"Please, call me Brandon. This is a meeting between friends, okay?"

"Okay," Rachel replied, nodding.

"Sometimes we make the mistake of sharing too much information with other people. When we do that it's like we're dumping our issues on others. I'm not saying you shouldn't share your concerns with your close friends or even your family, but remember all things in moderation." He chuckled. "So, other than your issues with your son, you seem to be in a good space. Am I right?"

"Yes, I'm good. I'm happy and I think I may have met someone. At least, I like him. I'm not sure if he likes me or not."

"I'm sure if you like him, then he probably already has noticed you. Speaking of meeting someone, what can you tell me about Hannah Steele?"

18

Rachel smiled as she entered her bungalow. When she opened the door, pleasant odors reminded her of contentment. Her apartment was warm and inviting, her very own happy place. The informal meeting with Dr. Mickens had given her peace of mind. She was ready to clear the air with her son and she was ready to explore a friendship with August. Changes the past months brought amazed her. She was, for the first time in a long time, actually happy.

The chiming of the clock in her bedroom reminded her of her dinner date with August in the dining room. Rachel studied herself in the mirror.

♦

Rachel's eyes zeroed in on August sitting at a nearby table. He got up as she approached and pulled a chair out for her to be seated.

"You look beautiful," he said.

"Thank you for having such an observing eye," she teased.

August smiled at this woman who intoxicated him.

They walked to the serving line and selected their food. After they placed their food on the table, August returned their empty trays to the tray rack. He found it almost impossible to contain his joy. He liked Rachel a lot. Life had taught him to edit his thoughts and not ride the winds of chance, but he was ready for a meaningful relationship. When he was alone in his bungalow, there were times he contemplated marriage again.

"I've missed you the past couple of days," August told Rachel. "I wondered if I did or said something to upset you. I even left a message on your cell phone and your answering machine."

"No , I'm not upset with you, August. I just had some issues that required a great deal of my attention. I heard your messages. I'm sorry I didn't get back to you until this evening. How have you been. And how's your daughter and those precious grandchildren?"

"I'm better now that I know you're good. And my daughter and the grandkids are doing fine. The twins will probably visit this weekend. They want to come and shoot pool with me in the game room." August laughed. He didn't pressure Rachel to go into detail about what was going on in her life. Instead, they laughed, talked, and enjoyed their meal. He found it impossible to keep his eyes from studying every inch of her face, her sensuous lips. He wondered how it would feel to kiss them. This woman made him feel like he did when he met his wife.

August smiled as he remembered his beloved wife and their life together, over thirty years before the Lord called her home. Debra would want him to find love and happiness again.

He and Rachel had finished dinner, and the table had been cleared.

"Let's move to a more comfortable area," he suggested.

August helped her from her chair. They walked together, stealing glances at each other like teenagers, except they were *antique teenagers.*

August opened the door into the lounge. Only two other people were in there. They talked for hours.

19

Karen pulled into the parking space next to her father's car. It was time to put Walter's memories to rest, time to think about life for herself and her children. She was terrified. Would God allow another tragedy to occur?

Her father had unwavering faith. He loved the Lord. He had lost his baby daughter, his beloved wife, and he grieved for his son-in-law who was like a son, but his faith remained solid as a rock. Never did she ever hear him blame or question God. Her mother had the same type of faith. Karen wished she could say the same thing about her own faith. Walter's death had jolted her, made her question God and her trust in him.

August was her rock after Walter's tragic death. Now she was at the point where she felt it was time to pick up the pieces of her life and live again. Could a man like Seth Winston be her chance at a new beginning? They shared similar life experiences with him being a widow and single parent the same as Karen.

According to her father, Seth's wife had died of cancer. They had one child, an eleven year old son named Jefferson. A warm feeling flooded her body thinking about Seth, but then a pang of guilt consumed her. Was she being disloyal to Walter's memory? Seth's face materialized in her mind. She *liked* him.

♦

The twins hopped out of the car and rushed up to their grandfather's bungalow. They loved the visits with him. They had made friends with Jefferson, Seth's son, who was there many times the twins visited. Jefferson was eleven, a year younger than the twins. He was energetic, and an excellent pool player. The pool stick was almost as long as he was tall but he was a master at the game.

The twins and Jefferson shot pool every chance they got. "Jefferson, the only reason you're so good at pool is because you're here all the time and you can practice," Samella said.

"Whatever," said Jefferson. "I'm just a pool shark." He laughed.

The twins made their way to their grandfather's bungalow and knocked on the door. They heard him and waited anxiously for the door to open. They rushed in and threw their arms around his waist.

"Hello, Granddad! How are you?" each child asked.

He embraced them in return. "I'm good now that I see the two of you. Where's your mother?"

"Here I am," Karen answered, appearing at his door.

"Karen, sweetheart. You're beautiful, did you do something different with your hair?"

"Do you like it, Daddy?"

"Yes, I do. It's pretty."

"Thanks, Daddy. I'm letting it grow out, and I got highlights in it."

Karen was pleased with her father's reaction. She wondered if Seth would like it. "The weather is turning cold. That North wind reminds me that winter is with us." She took off her coat and hung it on the coat rack along with Samuel's and Samella's coats.

"Yeah, we may have a rough winter. It's getting cold already and it isn't officially winter yet."

"Granddaddy, can we go and shoot some pool?" the twins echoed.

"First things first," August said. "Aren't you two supposed to be showing me something?"

"Yes, wait, let me run back to the car," Samuel said. "I forgot to bring my report card in."

"I have mine right here," said Samella, pulling a crumpled piece of paper from out of her purse backpack. "I made all A's and two B's."

"And I made two A's and three B's." Samuel ran out the door to go get his report card.

He returned minutes later. "Here, see," said Samuel. "Oh, and my team won our soccer championship. I have to bring the trophy I got the next time I come or when you come to our house."

"Okay, sounds good. I'm so proud of you," August said, giving a high-five to his grandson and a big hug to his granddaughter.

After enough time had been given for examination and praise, August told the twins, "You can go shoot pool. You both deserve it. You might see Mr. Winston's son in the hallways somewhere. I know he was here earlier. He might still be," August said.

"Is it alright, Mama. May we go now?" They asked.

"Yes, just remember to be polite. No running up and down the halls, you might bump into an older person and cause them to fall, so be careful," Karen warned.

"Yes, ma'am," Samuel said. "Come on, Samella." The twins took off out of the bungalow and into the adjoining area that would lead them to the other side of the building without them having to go back outside.

"Father, you seem in such a cheerful mood. It's because of Rachel Banks, isn't it?" Karen asked after the twins left.

"All I can say is I like her," August told his daughter. "But is it that apparent? Some of the fellows have been teasing me about her. They claim I smile like a Cheshire cat when I see her."

August and Karen grinned.

139

"I'm happy for you, Daddy. You deserve to have love again."

"You know, Karen, life is unpredictable. I never imagined life without your mother. When your mother died I was so unhappy. I didn't believe I would ever be happy again, but I am. I'm glad you convinced me to move here to be near you and the twins. And now I've met Rachel. Yep, I'm happy, Karen."

"I think she feels the same way about you, Daddy."

"I hope she does. Oh, before I forget, Seth asked me if I thought you might be interested in helping the planning committee set up the annual Thanksgiving bash. I told him you were good at planning things, especially being an elementary grade teacher, you know how to do stuff like that."

"Oh, Daddy, I don't think I'm that good at planning stuff."

"Oh, but you are. You may not see it, but I do."

Karen felt herself blush at the mention of Seth's name. She didn't know if her father noticed or not. If he did, he didn't say anything about it.

"He's probably still in his office. He had just called me a few minutes before you arrived, inquiring if you had gotten here yet."

Karen felt her heart beating rapidly. Her chest tightened. Just hearing his name affected her.

"Come on, I'll walk you to his office. I'm going to go watch the children shoot pool. May even play a couple of games with them. I've taught Rachel a few of my pool tricks," August said, his face deepening a shade.

August closed and locked the door to his bungalow and walked his daughter to Seth's office.

Arriving at his office, August knocked, waited on Seth to tell him to come in, and then stuck his head in Seth's office.

"Evening, Seth. I told Karen you wanted to see her."

Seth immediately stood from behind his desk and walked around it to where August stood. Looking past him, he saw Karen.

"Well, I'm going to the game room to watch the children shoot pool." He gave Karen a quick kiss on her cheek.

"Karen, come in. It's good to see you."

"Hi, Seth," Karen blushed.

"Please, have a seat." Seth motioned Karen to the chair across from his desk, and he swiftly returned to his chair. He did not want to stand a minute longer, afraid she might see how she effected every part of his body as he felt the growing tightness in his jeans.

Karen sat down. The loud beating of her heart seemed to drown out his voice. She had heard of women fainting, but she had never fainted. Yet, this man made her head spin until she felt dizzy.

"Are you alright? Your face is flushed."

Karen couldn't believe what was happening, "I'm...I'm good," she said, hoping he didn't see how nervous he made her. "Soooo, what is it you want me to help you with?"

He picked up a folder from his desk and handed it to her.

"This is my second year as the director of Senior Villas, but it's my first time planning a holiday festival for Thanksgiving and Christmas. I thought the best way to do it would be to form a committee to come up with ideas. That's where you come in. I want you to be on the committee."

Karen's eyes were fixated on Seth's full sensuous lips. She wondered about the softness of them as he opened and closed them or how they would feel as they engulfed hers.

"Karen. Karen?" he called her name.

She had no defense. She found Seth Winston appealing. The sound of his voice startled her, dragging her back to the moment.

"I'm so sorry, what were you saying?"

"I said, I wrote down some ideas for a holiday festival. I want to know what you think. It's all in that folder."

Blushing, she looked at the folder she held in her hands. Looking at the contents, she soon looked back up at Seth. "I would be delighted to work with you."

Karen decided at this point to meet the situation head on and see where it would lead.

His body had gained control. Seth got up from his chair and walked to her. Placing his hand on her shoulder, he snatched it back as an electrical current literally ran through the both of them.

"Did you feel that?" he asked.

Karen lowered her glance but said nothing.

Seth stepped to her, his heart pounding against his chest; he wanted to feel her in his arms. He paused after hearing someone approach his office.

"How are your plans coming along?" August said, stepping into Seth's office.

Seth stepped back as Karen stood up from her chair when her father entered.

"We were just going over them," Seth said.

"Don't let me interrupt you. Karen, I came to tell you the kids and I are going back to my place. We're going to order pizza. Seth, is it okay if Jefferson comes with us?"

"Sure. He likes hanging with Samuel and Samella when they come visit." Seth reached in his pocket and removed his wallet .

August observed Seth's actions and August raised his hand. "No need. This is my treat."

This time when August left out of Seth's office, Seth closed and locked the door. Karen watched in silence, not sure what he was doing.

Seth, remaining quiet, but with desire sparkling in his eyes, walked over to Karen, and hungrily pulled her out of her seat and into his arms. There was no resistance on her part. Passion rushed through them like a powerful electrical surge as their lips made contact.

He was so hard. When he pressed against her stomach, he became embarrassed.

Karen's body ached. Her nipples hardened as her body pressed against his. All the years of forgotten and denied passion broke loose like a mighty rushing river after the floodgates were lifted.

Seth wanted to drag her to the floor, rip away her clothes, and ease the burning need that consumed him.

Karen whimpered. She couldn't recall such an intimate drive ever existing in her, not even with Walter. Part of her told her she needed to stop what was happening, but she didn't want to stop it.

Suddenly, Seth pulled back from her as if he had been struck by someone. Gently, he guided her back into the chair that had held her before the riptide of passion consumed them.

He then walked back to his chair behind his desk, grateful for concealment.

They were speechless for several moments.

Their bodies reacted as if it had encountered a head on collision.

Karen grabbed a hand full of tissue from off his desk and dabbled at her eyes.

"Karen? Are you all right? I'm sorry. I didn't mean to—"

"It's not you, Seth. It's me. I'm just a little confused, that's all. It's...it's been such a long time," she said, beginning to allow her tears to fall.

Seth got up again and walked over to Karen. Reaching down, he took hold of her hand and led her to the dual set of chairs on the other side of his spacious office. Sitting next to her, he clung to her hand. "Karen, please don't cry, forgive me. I was overzealous. I shouldn't have." He cradled her in his arms.

"You have nothing to be sorry about. I was as much fault as you. I wanted you as much as you wanted me," she sobbed. What happened to us?"

"You already know the answer to that question. There's an attraction between us, a deep attraction. Our mouths can deny it all we want, but our bodies reacted to the real truth of what's going on between us," he said tenderly, looking into her eyes. "Our painful experiences are throwing up barriers, a self-protective mechanism. I don't know if you did, but I recognized it the first evening we spent together," he whispered.

"I'm just confused and I'm frightened, Seth. I don't know if you can understand how much losing Walter hurt me. I can't go through that again."

Seth looked into space. "I definitely understand. It was difficult seeing my wife, Rebecca, fight to stay alive, but her pain was too unbearable," he said, almost in tears himself.

Seth got up from his seat, walked to his desk, and returned with the folder.

"What do you say we allow the air to clear and our emotions to settle down a bit. Come on, tell me some ideas you have for the holiday festival."

Karen agreed with Seth's change of pace. She needed this intermission so her body, mind, and emotions could relax.

20

Rachel sat in her apartment recalling her conversation with Brandon Mickens. She was still surprised their paths had crossed again after so many years.

"Face your issues, admit your mistakes, except the consequences." Those were some of the words of advice Dr. Mickens had given her all those years ago, and he advised her all these years later to do the same thing. Hopefully, this time she would be able to follow his advice so she could release the hurtful hold of the past.

Rachel picked up the phone and called Luke. "Luke, I need to talk to you. Can we meet someplace where we can talk without interruption?"

'What happened, Ma? Did Seth do something?"

"No, honey, it has nothing to do with your brother. This is about you and me." She heard Luke suck in a deep breath.

"Okay, if you want to make sure we have privacy, then the best place would probably be here, at my office. Unless you want to go to a restaurant, grab a bite, and talk there," Luke suggested.

"No, your office would be best and I'm not hungry anyway. I'll see you in about half an hour. Is that good?" Rachel asked.

"Yes, half an hour is good. I'll close out some of these reports I was running. I should be done by the time you get here."

"Okay, I'll see you soon," Rachel said, ending the call.

♦

She pulled into an almost deserted parking lot outside Luke's office building. Once inside, she pushed the elevator button to the fifth floor. When she stepped off the elevator and the doors opened, Luke was standing on the other side. She observed him as she walked toward him. He was the spitting image of his father.

Rachel prayed she would remember what Dr. Mickens told her—*don't try to negate the situation, just take responsibility for your part in the failed relationship.*

Luke stepped to his mother, embraced her, and gave her a quick peck on her cheek. "Hi, Mama."

"Hello, Luke."

"Come with me," he said, leading her into his office.

Rachel and Luke talked for the next three and a half hours. She poured out her heart and soul to him, explaining everything that had transpired with his father, with David, with his brother Seth, and with her.

"Luke, son, I know our relationship has been repressed most of your life. The fault is all mine. I take full responsibility."

Rachel took her time and explained why it had been difficult to accept her son's gestures of affection. Luke sat attentively as his mother talked.

"When I married David, I was young and naïve. I had the idea that I could control life. David was in the Marine Corps. It was World War two. I feared he would be killed so I encouraged him to get out of the Marine Corps and join the Merchant Marine because I believed he would be safer. But your father didn't agree with me; he loved the Corps. He wanted to defend his country. Again, I cried, begged and intimidated him endlessly until he gave in and joined the Merchant Marines.

The Merchant Marines is not an official branch of the military, but they assist in various missions. If a need exists, instead of an official branch being called to respond, the merchant marines answer that particular assignment."

Rachel burst into tears, placing her head in her hands. "Oh, God, the irony of what happened still haunts me to this day."

Luke moved closer to his mother. He loved her so much, and her anguish affected him.

"David's ship was struck by a bomb. All on board were killed. I felt guilty. Had God punished me for leading my husband to go against what he wanted to do, which was be a Marine, by taking David's life?"

Tears settled in Luke's eyes as he listened.

"When my father, a rigid military man himself, discovered what I'd done, he was beyond angry with me. I don't think he ever forgave me for what I did."

Rachel tried to contain her tears but it was impossible. Luke took his handkerchief from his pocket and dried his mother's eyes.

"I robbed Seth of his father and lost the respect of my father. Three years later I met and married *your* father. I was happy that Seth had a father figure in his life. But your father wanted a child of his own, but I said no, because of my guilt. No amount of begging or intimidation changed his mind; he wanted children. Because I loved him, I gave him what he wanted, a baby—a son. You. Luke, your father was so happy when you were born. I felt like he neglected Seth after you were born. But it was all in my mind. He loved Seth just as much as he loved you. But, Luke, honey, guilt is a terrible enemy," Rachel said meekly. "I needed to blame someone for what had happened and for what I'd done so I blamed you, my innocent child."

Luke continued wiping his mother's tears away.

Rachel's body shook. "I kept you at a distance. I saw your heart break. How could I do what I did to you. Luke, please forgive me, son. I love you and I'm so very proud of you."

"Don't cry, Mother. I forgive you. I know you love me. Sure, when I was a kid, I would take my anger and frustration out on Seth because of the way you treated me. I thought you didn't love me, that you hated me. I told Seth that I hated him because he took your love from me. I encouraged some of my friends to call him names. We would laugh at him, call him nigga, and all sorts of ugly names until he would run off crying. It hurt me later, because he and I had been close up until then. As far as I know, Seth never told anyone about the way I treated him."

Rachel couldn't believe what she heard. It amazed her. For the first time, she realized how confused her son had been, and it was all because of her.

"I hated the way I treated you and Seth after Daddy died. Not resolving guilt robs one's soul," Luke said. "Thank God for Megan. She's a good wife. For years, she begged me to clear the air and mend the rift between me, you, and Seth, but I was afraid I'd lose the little love you had for me. I wanted to ask Seth's forgiveness a thousand times but I just couldn't. Because of me holding on to the haunted memories of my past, Megan and I are having problems. I know it's because of my unresolved issues. She wants to have children, but I can't, Ma. I feel incapable of loving a child or being loved. I don't want a child to feel the way I did," he cried.

"I'm so sorry, Luke. Lord knows I am. Please, son, please forgive me. I love you so much."

Mother and son buried their heads into each other and embraced. Releasing the guilt of the past felt liberating for both of them.

Luke walked his mother to her car and gave her a kiss on her forehead. He stood in his driveway, watching his mother until she disappeared up the street.

The storm that threatened to keep mother and son apart for years had dissipated. Rachel and Luke had made peace and mended fences.

21

Seth was surprised when he received a phone call from Luke telling him he wanted to stop by his office for a brother to brother talk. It had been weeks since they last spoke, which wasn't unusual for them. Seth figured all Luke wanted to do was come lecture him about their mother and voice his objections to her living at Senior Villas. He didn't want to entertain Luke and his foolishness. Quite the opposite. Seth often wished he and Luke had a better relationship.

There was a knock on Seth's office door. "Come in."

The door opened. Luke entered, looking quite anxious.

"What's up, brother? How's life treating you?" Seth inquired, standing up and greeting his brother with a hug.

"I've been better," Luke replied.

"Have a seat. You want something to drink like soda, coffee, water? Maybe something stronger?"

"Nah, I'm good."

"What's on your mind?"

"Look, Seth, so many times over the years, I've wanted to ask you to forgive the way I treated you when you were younger. Me and my friends called you out of your name and bullied you, but the truth is I was jealous and confused. We started out being close. You were my protector. You remember when I'd crawl into your bed when I heard a strange noise or there was a storm." Luke remembered his vulnerability.

Seth cracked a smile. "Yeah, I do."

"Then there was the cute girl who moved next door to us. I was mad because she chose you instead of me," Luke grinned. "Remember, she liked your hair, all your big curls. It was all the girls talked about when they realized you were my brother."

Seth chuckled lightly at the memories his brother resurfaced. He knew it must have been hard for Luke to come and open himself up like this, but Seth was sure glad he had. He continued listening.

"I regret the way I treated you and Mother after father died. There were times I felt he favored you. He adopted you after he and Momma married, but he treated you more as his biological son," Luke said.

"It's all good, Luke. You're my brother. I love you and I do forgive you."

Luke continued pouring out his feelings. Please forgive me, I was also wrong about Mother. She's blossomed since living here. She and I met earlier today and had a heart to heart talk. I believe our relationship is back on track, too. That's why I wanted to clear the air between me and you." Luke waited for his brother's response.

Seth answered Luke by getting up from his chair, walking over to his brother, and both men hugged one another, fighting back their man tears.

◆

After Luke left his office, Seth sat thinking about Karen. Without any provocation his body responded.

There was a knock on the door. Seth opened the door. There stood his mother.

"Hello how's my favorite girl?" Seth asked. "Come in and make yourself comfortable, I was about to pay you a visit. There are several things I need to talk to you about," he said.

"Do you want something to drink?"

"I'd like a bottle of water." She sat in a chair facing her son.

"Mother, Luke came to see me today. We had a brotherly talk."

"That is a blessing. Thank you, God."

"Yeah, and he apologized for the hard time he and his friends gave me. I honestly had let the past stay in the past, but I'm still happy we buried the hatchet and we're friends again...brothers," Seth concluded.

"Honey, that's wonderful," Rachel almost cried at hearing the news that her sons had reconciled.

"Momma, there's something else I wanted to talk to you about."

"What is it, Seth?"

"It's about Karen."

Rachel smiled. She knew her son had developed feelings for August's daughter.

"What is it, Seth?"

"Ma, I think I'm in love with her and I'm terrified. What if something happens to her as it did with Jefferson's mother. I lost a wife and he lost his mother. My feelings for her make me want to hurl caution to the wind. Then I think about Rebecca and how she suffered. Do you know how hard it was watching her suffer, knowing how much she wanted to live? How much she wanted to be here to see our son become an adult, to see him graduate from high school, go to college, get married and have children?" Painful memories slashed through his chest.

"Why must life be so complicated, why can't it work out as we planned? "He sighed.

"Life is not cut and dried, Seth. There will always be highs and lows. But we must trust, have faith, let go, and let God," Rachel said, smiling lovingly at her son. Years of mistakes forged this knowledge.

"I know Karen is frightened just like me." Seth walked to a window in his office that viewed the parking lot. Trees were bleak, stripped for winter, just like his emotions were stripped.

"Maybe we should let things stay as they are and raise our children, avoid any more pain." Seth turned and looked at his mother, listening for her advice.

"It's strange when I think of your question. You see, when I was young I thought I had things worked out, had them under control." Seth hung to his mother's every word. "The older I become the more I realize life is like a game of blind man's bluff."

Seth's brows furrowed. "Huh, what's blind man's bluff?"

"It's a game similar to tag where one of the players is blindfolded. The blindfolded player has to catch another player to tag him but you can only use your hearing and speed to catch the other player. No peeking." She grinned. "After your father died, I was afraid to venture out. Fear gripped my heart, until I met Harold. He taught me how to love again. Now I hope to develop a relationship with Karen's father. And as for you, I want you to be happy again, too, Seth. You deserve it. Life must be lived. Have faith in God, and know that love keeps you in the game although you may be blindfolded."

22

Hannah sat in her kitchen finishing up the last of some paperwork for the senior's group. The group had proven to be a godsend for the seniors who attended. There is no manual with instructions on how to grow old, graciously and reasonably happy, but this group helped.

Support groups can provide comfort as well as the answer to many problems seniors face. They can be a safe environment where seniors can feel comfortable making friends, sharing information, and having a positive outlet.

Over the months, Hannah's relationship with Alvin continued to improve, and she was at a happy place in her life. Whenever Alvin called she gave him her undivided attention.

Rachel's life was playing out like a Cinderella story for the antique teenager. She had met her Prince Charming when she met August. *Romance is possible as long as you think it's possible. Sometimes the senior lady may have to shake a few trees and beat around some bushes to locate Prince Charming,* she thought.

She remembered Hannah's line of questions. "How old are you? Are you married? If their answer is no, she took out her ink pen and pad, and asked the third question. "May I have your phone number?"

Hannah had talked to MaryLou. MaryLou was excited because she had met a male friend whom she really liked. She was shy about the idea of having a relationship again, but then she reminded herself that *this is no dress rehearsal and this day will not repeat itself.*

Seth visited the senior's group on several occasions and provided excellent information about living arrangements at Senior Villas.

Karen started dating Seth.

Hannah and Rachel became good friends and constant companions.

Dr. Brandon Mickens became one of the regular presenters at the senior meetings. A handsome man he was in Hannah's eyes with his sparkling daylight blue eyes and a head full of beautiful white hair.

The doctor and Hannah began spending time together. He helped her plan some of the senior group meetings. Their conversations and visits intensified. When she first noticed an attraction, she hesitated because he was not African-American.

Hannah's phone rang. It was Brandon.

"Hannah, this is Brandon."

"Good morning, Brandon," Hannah said, smiling broadly into the phone.

"I was wondering if you're not busy tomorrow evening if you would you have dinner with me. I'll be celebrating my eighty-second birthday. My children have reservations at Outback Steak House. I heard you say a time or two how much you like their food. So, would you help this old man celebrate his birthday?"

"It's a date," Hannah said, laughing into the phone.

"A date it is. I'll pick you up tomorrow at about five-thirty."

♦

The following evening, promptly at five-thirty, Brandon arrived with a beautiful bouquet of flowers. "I thought I would bring flowers. You know, do the entire teenage first date scene. After all, this is a date, right?" He smiled like a mischievous child.

Hannah nodded, blushed and ushered him inside, closing out the cold north wind.

"These are lovely," she said, "and so thoughtful of you," taking the flowers, inhaling their fragrance before placing them in a vase.

"Let's go, my lady. I hope this is the beginning of many such dates."

From that first official date, Hannah and Brandon started spending even more time together. They enjoyed going on walks together and watching movies, especially at his resident theater. Neither of them was interested in marriage, not at this point. Knowing there was someone to simply talk to for hours or a few minutes was wonderful, but Hannah's was not the only Cinderella story.

23

Karen occupied Seth's mind. Since their first encounter, they had been spending as much time together as their schedules would permit. He loved their engaging conversations. Karen had a way of making him feel alive. The more he was around her, the more he didn't want to let her go. The holidays were beautiful. Gatherings were heavily populated with friends and family. Seniors were at such a happy place.

It was settled, Seth had been thinking about it heavily for the last month—he was going to ask Karen for her hand in marriage. The wedding wouldn't have to be anything big and fancy, just a small wedding and a honeymoon—if she accepted his proposal.

His mother was right. *Nothing is set in stone so if you have the chance to catch a gold ring, catch it.* Karen was his *gold ring.* When he touched her, his body was consumed and everything about him was as hard as nails.

She desired him too. Seth could feel it in her body. Her hardened nipples were a giveaway. He felt them as his body merged into hers. Each kiss left them smoldering with desire.

Not giving in all the way to his sexual needs was proving to be more difficult. Sure, he tried to practice self-control.

Spending time in the presence of others helped the couple to keep their desires under wraps, but there were times when Karen and Seth pushed the limits.

Tonight, Karen and Seth's kids were spending the night with their grandparents. Seth and Karen took advantage of the situation to spend some alone time together.

Seth held Karen in his arms while simultaneously kissing, touching, and massaging her lovely body.

"I love you, Karen. This waiting is wearing me down. I ache when I think of you and my body reacts. I don't need anything but the minister, our family, and a few close friends. Will you marry me?" Seth waited for her reply.

She lay close to him, tingling from his intimate touch. Her body was a massive bundle of sensuous nerve endings.

Karen grinned, exposing her dimples. "Yes, yes, I'll marry you, Seth!"

Seth got up, walked over to the end table, and pulled a little box from its hiding place. He opened the black box at the same time he fell to his knees. He took the diamond ring from the box and placed it on her finger. It was a perfect fit. Seth grabbed her into his arms and kissed her passionately until tears brimmed her eyes. He felt moisture on his face. Love was aflame.

They fell asleep in each other's arms on the couch, not daring to tempt the bed in his spacious bedroom.

The following day, light from the morning sun beamed through the windows as Karen and Seth sat across from each other smiling like a couple of teenagers while eating breakfast.

"I thought about what you said, and I think a small wedding would be ideal. There won't be much to plan. Unless you have other ideas, you and Jefferson can move into this house with me and the twins."

"That's a good idea. Plus, I love this house. Or we can buy a brand new house. It's your choice."

"I think we'll hang around here for a minute. Plus there's plenty room for all of us. Samuel and Jefferson can share a room. I think bonding at their age is important," she said.

"I agree. I remember how close I was with Luke when we were young. I want that for Samuel and Jefferson." Seth added.

24

August and Rachel sat in the lounge. August faced Rachel. "Have you considered marriage again?"

Rachel wasn't surprised at his question. She'd actually thought about it a lot, especially lately after having met August. Not just about marriage in general, but marriage to *him*.

Addressing his question directly, she replied, "I have considered marriage. And I know even at my age that love is not limited just because we are older."

August saw on Rachel's face what he felt in his heart. His heart that had recessed after Debra's death was alive again and ready to be involved—with Rachel.

Rachel stepped forward and touched August's forearm. Her stomach felt like butterflies were flying around in it.

August's heart began to pulsate rapidly. Rachel was breathtakingly beautiful sitting in the chair smiling at him. The overhead lights added a special glow to her face, igniting fire in his groin. Until Rachel entered into his life, he had not realized just how alone and lonely he was.

Their friendship had stretched almost a year. They weren't getting any younger. August thought he'd strike while the fire was hot. The words came out of his mouth, words that had been buried in his heart. "Will you marry me?"

Rachel looked at him, eyes widened. Her pulse rate vaulted and she jumped with the spirit of a sixteen-year-old. It felt like her heart stopped. This was like a movie scene.

August pulled her up gently from her seated position, gathering her into his arms and smothering her with fiery kisses.

Some of the others in the lounge looked at the couple in awe.

"Yes, I'll marry you, August."

'She has agreed to marry me," he said breathlessly and a round of cheers exploded from the gathered group.

August and Rachel soon left out of the lounge. He walked her to her bungalow and he floated to his.

At his bungalow, he closed the door and placed his keys on the table, then picked up the wedding picture of him and Debra that he kept on the front room table. He kissed it lightly.

Next, he went to the closet. Pulling a small gray box from his closet, he sat in his favorite recliner, clutching the box in his hands.

Carefully, he opened it and wordlessly stared at the contents. He opened the beautifully sculpted piece. Taking some of the contents out of the container, he manipulated it between his fingers before sealing the container again.

Next, August slowly got up, grabbed his keys, and went outside and got in his car.

He drove until he arrived at his destination, a private and secluded spot he'd found one day when he was out exploring. It was nestled close to the Ohio River, not far from his neighborhood. He walked along the river bank. It was so peaceful and quiet. Even though winter was approaching, this evening, at this moment, he felt no chill in the air. Only the light beat of his heart.

Staring up into the moonlit sky and looking out into the heavenly night at the stars, he looked at the urn. With tears in his eyes, he slowly opened it, walked to the bridge and sprinkled the contents into the blowing wind, watching until the urn was empty. "Rest on, my sweet love, my dear Debra."

The End

About the Author

Evelyn Davis Dandridge Taylor Stamps is a native of Lexas, Arkansas. She served as a probation officer at Memphis and Shelby County Juvenile Court for over 35 years where her keen insight changed hundreds of lives. She was also an elementary schoolteacher.

She is a longtime member of Bethlehem Baptist Church where she serves on the Mother's Board. Taylor-Stamps serves as an active member of AARP (Chapter #2443), a member of the General Assembly Board at the Lewis Senior Center, and the Creative Writing Club. She is a comedienne, oral storyteller, and a member of the Memphis "Story Tellers" League. She is the author of 12 books and counting.

To arrange speaking engagements, purchase
signed copies, schedule appearances, book
events/conferences, or purchase books in bulk
CONTACT
Evelyn Taylor Stamps
evelyntstamps80@gmail.com
or (901) 474-9391

Made in the USA
Monee, IL
08 February 2021